# THE SPIRIT
# IN
# THE GLASS

JULIE HIGGINS

*For Maisy and Emma*
*XX*

# Acknowledgements

To my mum and all those we lost too soon.

To my dad, for making me a strong woman.

To my sisters, for teaching me how to argue.

To my children, my inspiration. I love you.

To Ron, my best friend and IT manager.

To Bex, my editor and guiding star.

To my friends, for without them this story wouldn't exist and my life would not be complete. Thanks for always being there and for believing in me.

To the future and many more adventures!

Lastly, to the NHS, for always being there.

# Author's note:

The novel you're about to read is set in Woolacombe, North Devon, a place of rugged cliffs, blue sea and golden sand. The countryside is beautiful and abundant with nature and the view of the red sun as it sets behind Lundy Island is unforgettable. It holds many special memories for me and my friends, and some of our madcap adventures and treasured tales feature in this novel.

Whether you're on your very own staycation with family or friends, or simply looking to be transported elsewhere, I encourage you to settle down with a glass of wine or cup of tea and enjoy!

The laughter, so out of place, seemed to break apart the clouds, revealing a patch of blue sky.

He heard it again, louder this time, intruding on his thoughts and challenging the dark feelings of despair.

Then he dared hope...

# CHAPTER 1

Windy Passage.

This would be home for the next three nights.

We all burst out laughing at the name, well, except for Mo. She scowled as her eyes fixed on the dilapidated house sign that was swinging precariously in the wind.

'Oh, I don't like the name,' she sighed, and we all agreed that it somewhat spoiled the ambience. Oh well, it was just a name.

'Wow, what a house! You've done well, Liz,' praised Karen as she edged the car up the steep driveway.

I was glad not to be driving, even more so seeing as a reverse hill start would be required. Memories of the near-miss last year at the lake house caused a sharp intake of breath from me and a sideways glance and smirk from Mo. What sort of architect designs a house at the bottom of a steep driveway then puts in state-of-the-art glass doors as a grandiose entrance?!

'Not a very good one, to put it politely, and it wouldn't get passed building regulations now!' Mo had scorned.

Memories! We had shared so many and had so many lucky escapes. I wondered if there were only so many times you could tempt fate before it all ended in disaster.

What was it about driveways? This year's house had an even steeper driveway leading upwards to an equally impressive entrance. The Victorian, wrought-iron porch was truly imposing, as was the original, solid wood door it housed which would hopefully make it somewhat safer.

'Oh, just look at the size of that doorknob,' purred Emma.

'**HANDBRAKE!**' we all shouted in unison. Last year's lesson was well and truly imprinted on the grey matter. No easy-press button, which had been the cause of the near calamity, just good old-fashioned mechanics.

The house was spectacular. We'd all viewed it online before booking, of course. It had been Liz's task this time to find a suitable retreat for our annual weekend getaway. This year was extra special as it was our tenth anniversary so we needed an extra special house. This one ticked all of the boxes.

'No plastic windows!' sang Karen in triumph. This was something she requested year-on-year along with copious amounts of butter and red wine.

'Is that the wind making your eyes water, Emma?' asked Mo. Emma was the youngest of the group and prone to outbursts of emotion which proved to be catching as both the house and the view had triggered a chain reaction.

We all stood in silence taking it in, our eyes watered as the wind swirled between us blowing our hair. It carried the sea's breath which was fresh and salty. Its coldness chilled our skin and heightened our senses. It whistled up and around the porch before clattering through the brass letterbox into the house.

Character, how do you define it? This house epitomised it. It wasn't just bricks and mortar. I could sense its personality. We all could. The persona that lingered within the stone walls and ancient rocks beyond reached out with an almost tangible vitality. We were rendered speechless which was most extraordinary.

It was a large Victorian semi. We always chose a property with four double bedrooms and at least two bathrooms, bladders not being what they once were. Good old Airbnb had come up trumps by the looks of it.

Roy had pointed out to me, mind you, whilst he was having a little nose at where we were staying, that there were a few bad reviews.

'Oh, don't start,' I'd pleaded, reminding him that reviews couldn't always be relied on. We'd been tricked by reviews on several occasions, luckily in a good way as we'd been pleasantly surprised after reading negative comments. 'I don't want to hear what the weather is going to be like either!' I'd groaned. The weather was his favourite doom and gloom subject, along with Brexit.

'I don't like this wind,' moaned Liz as she fought with the black mop of curls that billowed around her head, framing and enhancing her olive face and dark eyes.

'You look beautiful as always,' complimented Mo, and she was right.

'Don't worry,' reassured Emma, 'I've brought plenty of Frizz Ease.'

'Well you need to put more on,' laughed Amy.

Emma's hair, equally curly but twice as long, whirled like a golden halo around her head.

We'd recognised the house in the distance as we'd driven up the windy coastal road. It looked like it was built into the cliffside and promised stunning views.

Standing on the porch steps took your breath away, not entirely due to the wind either. It was like being in an infinity pool, talk about bird's eye view, the rocky cliffs and the sea seemed to emerge from nowhere. I love a calm, turquoise lagoon but the power and passion this grey, stormy sea evoked was exhilarating. Huge white-tipped waves crashing onto the rocks, black clouds looming down, you could almost see them supping up the sea to spill rain on us.

'I bet some ships have run aground down there,' said Amy. 'Imagine in the olden days running down to the wreckage on the beach to claim the smugglers' lost crates of wine and spirits.' It wasn't entirely clear what she was fantasising about, the visions of weather-beaten men or the alcohol!

'Trust you, Amy. I was just taking it all in,' said Liz, her reverie bluntly broken.

'It's so atmospheric, just like the moors. I almost prefer the bad weather,' she continued. Heathcliff for her.

Liz had such a calming effect on people, no wonder she was such a popular midwife with women wanting a natural birth. Shame she couldn't influence the weather. Her aromatherapy and reflexology skills were a real asset to the birthing unit and if we were lucky, like last year, she'd want a few guinea pigs to try out new treatments on.

The wind howled around us, picking up leaves and sweeping sand, only the tamarix trees dared to resist its strength with their bendy branches tested to the limits. The wind chimes were long gone by the looks of things, straggling strings hung like skeletons above the door. At least they wouldn't keep us awake at night. The big, old letterbox, however, rattled like a mouth of chattering teeth, acting as a vortex sucking the wind into the house.

'Brrr!' shivered Emma, still fighting with her hair.

'Like bad weather? Speak for yourself!' cussed Karen. 'Sun, sun loungers and cocktails for me!'

'Brilliant idea,' replied Rachel, looking pleadingly at Jill. 'How about you make me an Aperol Spritz?' she drawled in an Italian accent as Jill had been lucky enough to go to a wedding in Italy this year and we couldn't wait to hear all about it.

The seagulls squawked above, soaring on the wind like kites.

'Oh damn!' cursed Karen. 'Look at the mess on my car.'

'It's supposed to be good luck,' said Mo. 'Hopefully we'll have won something on the scratch cards this year.'

'That's only if they shit on your head!' laughed Emma. 'Never mind cleaning cars, how's work, Rach? Bet you're glad to have a whole weekend without any calls!'

We all felt sorry for Rachel, as acting ward manager she took shit from above and below and now she had it on her car! Keen to make her promotion permanent, she tried to maintain the status quo so consequently filled in whenever and wherever she was needed. She had the organisational skills but was far too good-natured to be a manager.

Rachel didn't answer Emma. She was deep in thought dusting off her car's gleaming paintwork. 'It was a waste of time washing it,' she cursed as she wiped the bonnet which appeared to be covered in sand.

'Oh, it's not sand,' she announced, looking at the fine, red dust covering her shammy leather.

I had a strong feeling of déjà vu as I noticed the red, shiny coating on the bushes around us. I had an eye for detail which was one of my best qualities, along with the ability to waffle and sound intelligent. It was my imagination that could get out of hand. My spontaneous response was both academic and flamboyant and not wholly out of character.

'The wind is most definitely southwesterly and judging by the strength of it you've got a coating of fine Saharan sand from the very desert itself,' I declared.

The weatherman had said the same thing this time last year if I remembered correctly. Roy had moaned about the orangey-red dust on our caravan. Weather again.

'I can just see you as a weather girl, Julia,' piped up Jill.

Maybe we'd be lucky this year and win something on our lottery syndicate, I hoped, noticing a shiny, black cat sitting on the gate. Its eyes glistened like emeralds. It, too, had a red tint on its coat. Most peculiar. Ginger tomcat probably got at its mother. Still, it was strange for a cat to be out in this weather. It was either brave or stupid like us.

Who would have ever thought that it was the middle of May? The jet stream had a lot to answer for. It was like the bloody middle of winter!

As the arduous task of unloading the two cars began, I looked up at the house towering above us. Something caught my eye in the neighbour's window and I wasn't the only hawk-eye.

'There's a curtain twitcher, ladies,' whispered Mo. 'Don't look now!' she mumbled, grinding her teeth and sealing her lips. 'Far left, top window.' Her eyes flicked upwards, her head too.

We all looked up simultaneously as the curtain closed.

'Oh, that was so obvious!' she laughed.

'Well, I don't know why you're whispering. As if they'd be able to hear you in this weather!' scoffed Amy.

'Never presume,' I lectured, remembering what had happened at the staff meeting before we realised that Matron, our boss, could lip read. A formal warning was way over the top, we'd all agreed. Poor Karen. She'd left and got a job as an infection control nurse after that.

'As long as we've not got a Peeping Tom on our hands, I'm happy,' said Jill.

'Well, I don't care actually,' I stated with defiance, thinking about my new tummy control costume and the pounds I'd shed on this new vegan diet. 'He can look as much as he likes.'

'That's exactly what I say to Mick these days!' Jill laughed.

'Surely it's better touching but not looking when you get to our age,' argued Mo.

My eyes were drawn to looking up at the house again. It seemed to dominate my thoughts. The more I looked, the more I noticed. It was painted in the drabbest colours, moulding itself into the rock face like it was trying to hide, quite the contrary to how I'd initially perceived it.

Indeed, it was certainly quite ugly despite its unique features. That age-old cliche popped into my mind, dare I say it, I knew I wouldn't as it was too on the nose, but it was exactly how I imagined a haunted house to look. Now there's a devious idea if ever there was one. Something told me that this was going to be a weekend to remember.

After the grand tour and a lot of oohing and aahing, the process of room allocation would begin. After ten years together, who shared with who was pretty much set in stone. We all knew each other's preferences, dislikes and unfortunate habits. On this occasion, the snorer, or the worst snorer at least, opted for a room on her own. This room, in fact, wasn't shown in the house details, it was an extra bedroom downstairs off the hallway.

'Brave woman who dares go there!' piped up Rachel in a ghoulish voice. 'Fine Jill, if you like it, but it looks a bit lonely in there.'

'Oh, it's chilly,' said Emma, with a shiver.

'You're always cold,' teased Amy. 'Poor circulation is the most likely culprit, it helps if you exercise more!' We all knew that Amy didn't like anything cold or stiff on a weekend away. She had enough of that at work.

'Well Karen, do you think it's all alright?' asked Liz tentatively.

Karen's forte was infection control. She'd fallen on her feet since she left the birthing unit, risen right up the ranks. To be honest, she was always a bit of a pencil pusher and audit freak. She loved inspections, even requesting to work if she got tipped off that CQC were coming. The rest of us had always wanted to hide. Emma quite literally hid in the sluice that one time. Well, the less said about that the better. Anyway, Karen's new job suited her perfectly and meant she'd have ample opportunity for scrutinising, reviewing and writing guidelines. So it all worked out for the best in the end, thanks to Matron.

We all knew she'd find something to complain about, dust or dirt at the very least. We all hoped she hadn't brought the white glove this year, that was too over the top.

'Complaints keep standards high!' she'd bleated many times before.

There had been some embarrassing moments in restaurants over the years, funny how she never complained about food going off in her fridge. Her mother had brainwashed her to have a 'waste not, want not' attitude and it was good advice on the whole. I'm not too sure about continuing to eat things until they give off a smell though, well, apart from cheese. Amy, of course, agreed with her and that was something to treasure, as those two rarely agreed on anything.

'A glass of wine and it will all be fine,' was Amy's motto.

'What's the science behind that?!' we'd queried on many occasions.

'Alcohol kills the germs!' she'd slurred.

'And the brain cells!' I'd said in response.

'Disgusting, look at all those woodlice on the windowsills. I hope there is not an infestation,' Karen said, screwing up her face. We could tell by her mannerisms that she was building up to a verdict and we all knew what it would be. In her most official voice, she announced that, in her opinion, the house hadn't been thoroughly cleaned. 'Standards not met!'

We mouthed the words with her as it was the same every year.

'I'll write a review when we get back. Three stars out of five!' she said nudging what looked like mouse droppings with her toe. Each year she hoped we'd get a refund or a money off voucher so she always complained. We were still waiting, though not with bated breath. Well, come to think of it, three out of five wasn't that bad.

'We will have to settle for a cup of tea and homemade cake as we've no other food or alcohol until the food delivery comes,' said Liz with a tone that suggested the world was coming to an end.

'Earl grey for me!' chirped Karen heading to the lounge.

As the kettle boiled, Mo started unloading the essentials box. That box had a story or two to tell, still going strong after ten years. It spent eleven months of the year stored in a garage protecting its wares until the next trip.

Only half a bottle of Disaronno survived last year. Karen had finally thrown away the vinegar which had lasted nine years, after reluctantly agreeing that it had separated and was not fit for consumption. She made a point of telling us, however, that it did a marvellous job of cleaning her windows.

There were fresh tea bags, of course, they'd never end up as leftovers, like wine which never survived longer than three days.

'I can't wait 'til the auction,' piped up Amy. 'I know there's gonna be loads of food left over come Monday. You've ordered too much again!'

We all knew she was right. She'd get her moment of glory on Monday morning when we auctioned off the leftovers between us and gave the money to charity.

'Sheer greed!' she muttered as she commenced her afternoon pilates. Alcohol loosens the joints as well as the tongue, I surmised as she put her toe to her mouth. Her fear of becoming stiff was definitely getting worse; I suppose it must be a mortuary assistant's worst nightmare. Thank goodness she had worn appropriate clothing this year. I had my fingers crossed that she'd also remembered to sort her bikini line. Being no wider than a kipper between the eyes, she was the one who needed exercise the least.

'Well, I didn't hear you say we'd bought too much alcohol, Amy!' said Jill.

'No, why would I?' she replied, huffing and puffing, 'I don't think we've got enough!'

'We're doing something a little different this weekend,' stated Karen as she came to get her tea. 'Wine tasting! I'm fed up with people saying they only like certain wines when I know damn well that most of us drink anything if the price is right!'

'I know she's trying to catch me out,' Amy whispered.

'I think we should do tea tasting as well,' said Emma, feeling brave. 'I'm sure you were drinking cheap tea from Tesco last year, Karen!' That was like putting a red rag to a bull and Amy lapped it up. Karen hated Tesco with a vengeance.

We'd started all those years ago with a modest shop from a budget supermarket. There was minimal scope for online grocery shopping back then but now we opted for a top-notch home delivery service of luxury food. We felt the expense was justified once a year and it was a reasonable price considering it sustained eight big eaters and drinkers over three days.

We had aimed years ago to make it an all-inclusive break. Year-on-year more things had been included. It was now certainly worthy of a gold star, if not four!

We all paid a modest amount into our joint account every month enabling us to have a fully paid weekend break once a year. That included accommodation, food, drink, trips out, lunches, sometimes an evening pub meal, even parking and petrol was accounted for. Jill was the treasurer and a damn good one at that. Jill was management material, if anyone was. In her role as a senior care assistant, her common sense and work ethic kept the ward ticking over. She was a whizz on the computer too. None of us could believe it when the boy from IT called her a dinosaur. After all, she'd summoned him to help me with the computer in the clinic. If she was a dinosaur what on earth was I?!

We knew for sure that we wouldn't need to spend a penny this weekend, unless, of course, you were one of the shoppers in the group. We had a few of those, although Mo's vice was the charity shops. We also had a T K Maxx junkie in tow, though I'm pretty sure she never bought her shoes there.

'Well, is the kitchen to your liking?' Liz asked Karen and Rachel as they were the cooks or 'chefs' as Karen liked to say. That was their main job for the weekend as they were good at it and enjoyed it, not to say that the rest of us weren't as good. Well, I'm not too sure about Jill actually after the boiled egg incident...

I had taken the blame with her, fighting off Karen with the burnt pan and comforting Amy who cursed that her chicken's eggs had been wasted. We'd all ended up inebriated that night after a supper lacking in protein and carbs as Mo had forgotten to put the potatoes on.

That incident had prompted organisation and job sharing. We now had official roles, fitting together perfectly like pieces of a puzzle. Eight different characters. Friends who had been together through thick and thin over the years. Teamwork, camaraderie, fun and an awful lot of hard work had been our life's blood. Work. That's where we had all met and stayed, apart from Mo, who had recently taken early retirement, and myself who had left on a whim. And for the time being, the less said about that the better.

'Yes, the kitchen is perfect. Well, almost...,' said Karen, remaining conservative. I sensed arguments were afoot. Thank the lord Brexit had been decided! The bickering and sulking almost ruined last year's break. It was strange how people with such differing opinions could be such good friends. We'd learned last year that none of us really liked freedom of speech unless it was what we agreed with. Who wants to be called a bad loser?! This year we'd all agreed, no politics and no bitching. We didn't consent to no arguing as we knew that would never happen.

'Nice oven and dishwasher,' said Rachel familiarising herself with the controls. 'Big knobs which I like,' she said, testing the ones on the oven. 'I have to put my glasses on if they're too small so I can see what I'm doing.'

We all laughed, Mo just raised her eyebrows.

'Don't encourage them!' she said to Amy, rolling her eyes.

'There's some jarred essentials here - pasta, rice, lentils,' Karen muttered. 'And sugar...the root of all evil!'

She blamed sugar for stealing her waist and giving her bingo wings. There was never a bad word said about butter unless, of course, it was unsalted.

No wine, unfortunately. The kitchen was always our favourite part of the house and where we'd spend most of our time. It was a big room with the dining area at the front of the house providing spectacular sea views from the huge bay windows. Emma strolled around admiring the ceiling rose and cornices.

'I love the wooden doors and the oak floor. I wonder if it's original?!' she queried.

No one was really listening, we were all sitting at the huge rustic table in the centre of the room taking in the views and sipping our tea. Raindrops glistened on the windows acting like fairy lights as a flash of lightning passed through them. We all counted aloud, only getting to three before the massive crackle of thunder sounded.

'Three miles! That's close,' said Amy, jumping up to check the church spire in the distance.

'We might get to see some firemen!' I chuckled, winking at Emma.

'Well, I never thought we'd get weather like this in May but anything is possible,' she laughed.

It was like looking down at a miniature village, the perfect house for nosey parkers and people watchers. Shame there were none of those here...

You could see the village pub, The Shipwreck, quite clearly nestled on the headland. That's where we were going for our supper.

'Were the roses here when we arrived?' asked Jill admiring the display in the vase in the centre of the table.

'Yes, a nice touch,' answered Liz. 'Make sure you put that in your review, Karen.'

'This cake is delicious!' purred Mo enjoying the cake made by Rachel's daughter.

'The best one we've ever had!' Amy said, raising her voice so Karen could hear.

'You're no judge, Amy, you don't usually eat cake!' Karen snapped.

Round one had just begun!

# CHAPTER 2

'Gosh! We've come a long way from our first trip,' said Liz. We all smiled, conjuring up memories of that weekend all those years ago.

We'd come back to the same place for our tenth anniversary, not the same accommodation though. I don't think you can call a tent accommodation, although maybe you can nowadays what with glamping and electric hookups. The motorhome had been lovely, reminiscent of childhood caravan holidays.

'The journey down in the motorhome was brilliant! A great laugh. I remember it being really comfortable as well,' said Amy. 'Karen was a damn skilled driver. It takes a lot of concentration, especially when certain passengers are helping themselves to Bacardi Breezers from the fridge. What lightweights we were back then!'

'I don't know how six of us fitted in that motorhome,' remarked Liz shaking her head.

'We were all a lot thinner and more agile. You lot would never get on that top bunk now and it definitely wouldn't take the weight,' Amy replied.

Nobody mentioned me and Emma in the tent. Some things were best left unsaid. At least the weather had been good, I thought as my face flushed. Some important lessons were learned that weekend for sure.

The first was to not drink alcohol on an empty stomach. The second was to not let Amy do the barbecue. Karen and Rach took on the cooking roles after that catastrophe, thank goodness.

Rachel played a starring role on that trip, as a former Girl Guide she'd erected the tent almost single-handedly. She'd set up the motorhome, even though it wasn't hers, and put us all to shame, especially Karen who didn't have a clue about anything other than how to keep the beer cool. Her feeble excuse had been that Rachel had been caravanning for years and was practical-minded, whereas she herself was an intellectual.

It's a surprise the trips continued after that weekend, as well as the friendships. I suppose it was a test that we all must've passed as our friendships only grew. We'd stuck together through thick and thin over the years, supporting each other through the highs and lows, admiring and praising each other as we built our families. Now some of us were welcoming grandchildren into the fold.

There had been a few arguments along the way, not many, but we'd all pulled through. I think we must all be very tolerant and compassionate. Why we couldn't be like that with our husbands was one of life's mysteries.

Tolerance and compassion, you certainly needed those qualities to work successfully within the caring profession and we'd all done well there. We could definitely hold our heads high with pride where our jobs were concerned. All still married to the same men as well. Now that's an achievement, never mind degrees and diplomas!

What a bunch, too good to be true? No, we were definitely not perfect, far from it, we all drank too much for one thing, but we were a great crowd and I'd never dreamed I'd have friends like this. But the greatest thing of all, true happiness, was my children, the meaning of life for me, Roy coming in a close second. Life was good and this weekend was just what we needed. I didn't think things could get much better. Well, at least not until the food delivery arrived brimming with wine, spirits and delicious food.

'We'd better go and help with the boxes,' I suggested, glancing at the driver who looked like he should be retired. Poor man, still working at his age and delivery driving as well - very stressful and definitely an essential service. Us lot often moaned about our jobs being stressful but I knew the rewarding, memorable moments and job satisfaction far outweighed the negatives.

'Stop dithering,' sighed Amy. 'He's probably working to top up his pension.' Bloody mind reader. I knew for sure, like me, she was thinking about getting the sauvignon blanc into the fridge. When she was on a mission she moved like the wind which was apt as it was blowing a gale that was beginning to sound more like a hurricane. I wondered if it was bad enough to be given a name? Storm Emma, perhaps, or Storm Julia?

'Christ! How long are you lot here for then?' the driver asked looking at all of the boxes of food and drink.

'Just the three nights,' we said in unison.

'I hope there are no substitutes,' piped up Karen. We all knew she was talking about the time they substituted branded tonic for 'cheap rubbish' as she'd put it. I was pretty sure that was what had prompted the wine tasting she was planning. I hoped they hadn't given us margarine instead of butter as that was a cardinal sin in Karen's eyes. Mind you, she has been muttering about going vegan - perhaps miracles really do happen?! I wondered if you could get vegan butter.

Jill, our accountant, fished out the pocket money purse and, along with our thanks, gave him a generous tip.

We made light work of putting everything away like worker bees buzzing and humming around the kitchen. 'I hope you've got some eighties music to play later, Emma!' said Liz twerking around the table. 'And Fleetwood Mac, of course.'

'You'd better get shaking this,' sang Amy, producing a silver cocktail shaker like a rabbit out of a hat.

Liz was the cocktail queen and we knew we'd be in for a treat this year. As it was a special celebration, we knew she'd go the extra mile and judging by all the spirits she'd lined up, alongside fresh pineapple, cherries, lemons and limes, we wouldn't be disappointed.

Amy opened the umbrella sticks and marvelled at the sparklers. Amy and I were the waitresses, toing and froing with drinks making sure no one had an empty glass. One of the most important jobs was making sure the drinks were strong enough and Amy was an expert at that. Nothing was ever wasted hence the use of last year's leftover Disaronno in the first cocktail of the day, Alabama Slammers.

Drinks in hand, the next phase of the inspection was about to begin. Hot tub here we come!

Having a hot tub was a prerequisite when choosing our accommodation. Even though most years we'd holidayed in the spring or early summer, the weather often let us down and this year was no exception. It was a big tub, situated on the decking at the back of the house.

'Oh, I'm not sure about those rocks,' scorned Rachel looking up at the cliff face. Her health and safety head coming to the fore.

'I wish I'd brought Mick's helmet for you,' laughed Jill.

'I prefer Gary's,' drawled Emma sucking on her straw.

'Here we go! Fruit juice has gone to her head already,' laughed Amy. 'These drinks are too weak. I'm going onto the wine as it's chilled enough now.'

'I've seen you drink it warm!' I said, rolling my eyes. Her glare was fervent.

'Yeah, mulled wine at Christmas.'

'I fancy a prosecco next,' announced Liz.

We'd never learned the lesson about mixing drinks, even after all the years together. I shrugged it off as another old wives' tale.


It was a steep, tiered back garden. The terraces looked neglected and were overgrown with weeds and bird droppings. Stone steps led up to each level and there was a rocky cliff behind. The grey rocks towered up and seemed to merge with the sky. A herring gull loitered on a rocky shelf looking for easy pickings.

I noticed what looked like a bird hide in the rock face in next door's garden. Prime place for bird watching and prime place for a Peeping Tom as it must have a perfect view of the hot tub. There were remnants of nests littered amongst the pink thrift growing on the ledges and more gulls swooped down eager to claim their territory.

'Don't feed the seagulls! We'll get mobbed,' warned Karen.

It was a scary-looking house from the back. Lack of sunlight made it drab and dismal, moss and lichen growing in the cracks like it held it all together. Dampness oozed like sweat from the porous stone making everything wet and slippery. We'd need to be careful that no one fell over, especially after a few drinks. There would be no nice view from this hot tub, apart from the stars above, at least we'd have a sparkling ceiling if the clouds blew over and we got a clear night.

The tub seemed to be in full working order and the water was clear according to Karen's assessment. We all agreed to try it out that evening when it was dark.

'It's always better in the dark,' said Karen.

'Speak for yourself,' laughed Emma.

'Please no talking about sex this year,' pleaded Mo. We all knew that rule would be broken along with many others. It was Mo herself that had dished out advice last year after a few wines. Fancy having to take two ibuprofen half an hour before sex! I would have thought it was contraindicated, being anti-inflammatory. Apparently not. Jill had agreed it works a treat.

'Remember that ultra-modern house with the fancy hot tub that was dirty,' two of us chirped together.

'Yes,' snapped Karen. 'I had to phone and complain before we could use it. We were chomping at the bit to try it out.'

Oh, but it had been worth the wait! What a shock we'd had when he appeared at the door. It was certainly a nice surprise. We must've interrupted his training regime. He was still in his gym kit, tight shorts and bare-chested, glistening with sweat.

The pushing and shoving that had taken place was shocking, we realised then how competitive we all were. It must have been our hormones, making the most of it as they knew they would soon be gone. That was the only time we'd ever seen Karen tipping dirt from the net into the tub the next morning. She's normally such a clean person.

We went inside as the skies opened up and the rain thrashed down again, hoping that a storm might clear the air and make way for better weather tomorrow.

'Oh shit,' scathed Jill, pulling a face as she sniffed the mess on the bottom of her shoe. 'Bloody cat shit!'

'I thought cats were supposed to be clean animals,' said Karen sarcastically to Amy. We were all dog lovers whilst Amy preferred cats and chickens. None of us lingered in the hallway. It felt colder there than outside, we headed to the window seat to warm up and take in the view.

'Good grief, you aren't gonna eat now, are you? We're having a pub meal tonight,' remarked Amy as Rachel and Karen raided the fridge for snacks. I knew the question was aimed at Karen by the way Amy's eyes bored into her back. She obviously resented the comment about cats.

'That's tonight! Besides, there's a method in the madness, we need to soak up some of the alcohol before we go out. Remember what happened last year?' Karen chastised, looking at me.

'Pop!' sounded the cork as Liz opened another prosecco in defiance.

When I looked at the table it was already laden with nibbles: nuts, olives, dips, crisps and breadsticks for dipping.

'I'll take them home for the chickens,' scoffed Amy pointing to the celery sticks that Liz had found as a healthy option. 'It's safe to wash the cucumber,' she added, winking at me as it was our inside joke. Was she hinting at cucumber batons?

'Yes, and I can bend down without any hassle!' I replied, rolling my eyes.

'This is the life!' purred Emma, relaxing on the window seat with her feet up, sipping a pink gin and tonic. 'I'll take our annual photo tomorrow. We can sit here in those beautiful dresses you purchased.' Her tone playful and sarcastic, provoking a dirty look from Amy.

I glanced at the worktop and noticed that we'd opened every bottle of spirit. We never learned. I didn't feel an ounce of guilt as I knew none of it would be wasted which was shameful in itself.

Time really does fly when you're having fun and today was no exception. Glancing at the antique clock on the wall I realised it was already seven o'clock. We'd been laughing, joking and drinking for two hours. Rachel had noticed too and was busily collecting up the empty glasses. Karen poured everyone a large glass of water as we were all rather tipsy. It was the same scenario every year. We would go overboard on the first night and there would be hangovers Saturday morning, which usually ensured that we would tone down the drinking somewhat.

Mo jumped up with a start, she'd fallen asleep. We all rushed upstairs in a mad panic to get ready. As I passed the bottom of the stairs, I smelt a strange odour. A whiff of camembert being carried by a draught from the fridge, perhaps. That's the only thing with French cheese.

'The table's booked for eight o'clock so we need to get a move on!' shouted Jill.

We'd scrubbed up nicely all things considered. A brisk walk in the fresh sea air was just what we needed to wake and sober us up.

The rain had stopped but we could hear the wind howling around the house, rattling windows and doors. Karen took the full force as she opened the door, losing grip of the huge doorknob. The heavy door slammed into the wall like an angry beast, just missing Amy.

Then nothing, silence, calm, stillness, the wind simply disappeared. That must be why it's called Windy Passage, I concluded as I shut the door behind us.

The sky looked menacing, the grey clouds were blackening as the light faded. The sun was disappearing, just its red outline around the clouds remained. It was the strange mist we were most intrigued by, appearing like smoke circles in the distance, slowly weaving around the landscape like a creeping vine. Insidious.

Amy and Karen took the lead, setting the pace. We all kept up this time. There was something else beyond the nip in the air and I was sure they all felt the same. We never walked this fast for one thing, especially not in heels. For some uncanny reason, no one dared look back at the house.

The sighs of relief came as we stepped into the pub, lapping up the warmth, the bright lights and fellow beings. Nothing like a fright to sober you up.

The Shipwreck didn't disappoint. It was just what I'd imagined and I knew the others were pleased judging by their smiles.

'We all deserve a strong drink after that!' said Jill marching to the bar with the purse. That was totally out of character for her so I reckoned that she, like myself, had been scared.

'Good excuse this time!' sighed Karen. 'I give up!'

Amy was already halfway through her order of a large chardonnay. She was the fastest walker, especially when there was a bar in sight, and I expect the brisk walk had given her a thirst. We sat quietly letting the wine work its magic, warming our throats and easing tensions.

The scare was soon forgotten as we admired the decor and original features of the 16th-century inn. They even had the log burner on which outraged Karen as it was May. Though the pub was busy, full of locals, tourists, and Friday nighters, the hustle and bustle of bodies soothed us.

Hunger soon led to impatience. The waitress had been beckoned over by a rude click of the fingers. The menus were passed around and we were ready to order before she could make her escape.

Mo got her words in first and it was the same as usual, 'Homemade lasagne with garlic bread, please.' She looked to see if Amy was listening before adding a side of chips.

Jill chose her favourite, ribeye steak with all the trimmings.

Liz was still browsing through the starters.

'Gosh! You're not having a starter after all those nibbles at the house?' Amy said loudly, provoking a snarl from a woman at the next table.

I had decided to be pescatarian today so I opted for the seabass, the catch of the day, caught locally and bought fresh from the nearby harbour. The others followed suit, apart from Karen who ordered green bean risotto.

'Blimey, there's a lot of different beans in there,' remarked Amy nosing at the description. 'I hope you won't get wind,' she sniggered. Our eyes all rolled together and the sighs were all in harmony too. Talk about the pot calling the kettle black.

What a feast for the eyes when my dish arrived, a garden on a plate. Golden samphire surrounded the fish, piccolo tomatoes and violas made for a pretty garnish. The fish was cooked to perfection, crispy skin but moist inside, and the tiny potatoes were coated in a shiny sauce which turned out to be delicious. I was secretly pleased that there was no trendy foam, which reminded me too much of the spittlebugs in the garden.

Amy wasted no time devouring the huge shell-on prawns on her plate. Emma cringed as she watched her suck their heads between slurping big gulps of wine. She was unusually squeamish for a care assistant.

I didn't fare much better. I pulled the head from a prawn which unfortunately acted like the trigger on a water pistol. Thick pink liquid shot across the table splattering the white blouse of the woman that had snarled at Amy earlier. Was there some sort of official prawn etiquette? Was that why Amy was fervently sucking the brains out first? Emma gasped and put her hand to her mouth, maybe to hide a baulk. She then proceeded to scrape her prawns onto Amy's plate, 'I've decided I only like them ready-peeled.'

Attention soon turned to Karen who was making familiar mutterings and had not eaten very much. 'It's not creamy enough and they've cooked it for too long,' she mumbled.

'Is this what you want?' asked Amy, producing a pat of butter she'd swiped from another table.

'Get me two more, please,' pleaded Karen.

The meal was delicious, cooked to perfection. There's a lot to be said for gastropubs. We were pleasantly full and alcohol levels had been topped up. What more could we want?!

As soon as she'd polished off her meal, Amy propped herself up at the bar and was now in full flow chatting to the barmaid. She'd talk to anyone. I went to join her. The barman took my order as I eased onto the barstool. It was noisy but I could just make out the conversation Amy was having.

'Oh, it was empty for almost a year after the accident. Of course, police investigations take a while and tragedies like that put people off. The owner was shocked, as were the villagers, they seemed like such a nice couple.'

'What?! He actually died in the house?' asked Amy.

'Oh, yes! His partner, Lisa I think she was called, found him dead at the bottom of the stairs in the morning. Apparently, they'd had a bit too much to drink the night before and she'd gone to bed in a drunken state.'

Well, we've all done that, I thought to myself, and I think that was on the horizon tonight judging by the units we were clocking up.

'All hell broke loose the next morning when she found him in a pool of blood. Ambulances, police, all tearing around the village, the poor woman was hysterical.'

I gave Amy a dig in the side. She was so mesmerised by the story she hadn't noticed I was there. She pulled her stool closer to the bar, as did I. We both took huge slurps of wine, feeling that was justified considering what we were hearing. I shushed the bloke next to me.

'What had he died of? A broken neck? Fractured skull?' Amy asked. I tutted. Geez, she's not a pathologist.

'Please don't tell me he was bludgeoned...or stabbed?'

'Oh no, much worse. I think the coroner recorded it as catastrophic blood loss in the end. They think he was carrying a glass of whiskey up the stairs. He must have stumbled and dropped the glass before falling down the stairs. A shard of glass pierced his neck apparently. After a full investigation, I believe it was recorded as an accidental death. Imagine the mess! Five litres of blood in the hallway. Well, that's the volume for the average man. I Googled it.'
She looked troubled, well, upset I'd say. She rushed to serve a customer at the other end of the bar.

Amy had turned very pale and seemed at a loss for words, which was most unusual as she dealt with dead bodies daily at work. I wondered if it was the number of prawns she'd eaten and all the wine she had consumed. The barmaid finished serving the customer then returned to continue the story.

'He's buried in the churchyard on the hill. He was in his early forties, I think. What a waste of a life. Anyway, enjoy your weekend! I hope the weather improves.' She made a quick getaway into the kitchen before we could speak. That's put a damper on things, I thought as we both looked at each other.

'Hey, don't tell the others,' Amy pleaded. 'It'll only spoil things. Let's keep it to ourselves.'

We both downed what was left of our wines and went back to the table.

'One for the road?' asked Karen.

'No,' said Amy firmly. 'I think we should go back now.'

'Well, that's a first!' laughed Liz.

'I think she's got a stomach ache,' I whispered to the others, raising my eyebrows as I made the excuse.

'We all know what follows that!' Emma replied.

Into the darkness, we ventured. No one had thought to bring a torch, not even Rachel. The clouds had gone, revealing the starry sky that we'd hoped for. The mist still lingered, like a thick cobweb hovering just above the ground.

The wind had subsided, now just a refreshing welcome breeze. We could hear the sea, gentle lapping of the waves as they met the shore. The glow from the lighthouse on the headland shimmered in the distance like a giant lamp guiding us home. We trudged up the hill, arm in arm, and then we heard it, a high-pitched sound like a balloon going down. We all knew what it was, as we'd all heard it many times before.

'Get out and walk!' slurred Amy.

'Stomach ache gone?!' I managed to say, tears rolling down my cheeks.

'She must have a tight ass,' cried Emma.

The laughter continued up the hill to the house. We noticed a few curtains moving and lights coming on and someone opened their front door and tutted loudly. Poor neighbours, they must get fed up with rowdy holidaymakers.

'Oh my God! Someone's taking the piss,' said Rachel.

We all saw it together.

'Taken the P,' laughed Mo in hysterics. The wind must've blown part of the sign away. We were now staying at 'Windy Assage'.

'Most appropriate,' choked Karen, bent over double.

'Open the door!' cried Liz, 'I'm gonna wet myself!'

'I already have!' screeched Emma.

'Never mind! We're going in the hot tub anyway!' cried Jill with mascara running down her face.

Amy and I both stood still.

We'd both seen the two red eyes in the bedroom window next door before the curtains had quickly been pulled shut.

# CHAPTER 3

We entered the house in a mad frenzy, all racing for the loos apart from Amy who was muttering about weak bladders and pelvic floor exercises.

'There's a terrible smell in here,' moaned Jill, screwing up her face and pinching her nose as she went to the fridge to help herself to a cider. I think we both wondered if Amy's bowels were the culprit but we daren't say so as she was curled up on the sofa looking very sorry for herself. I went to the fridge hoping to solve the problem and any embarrassment.

'The camembert reeks! The smell must be blowing through to the hallway,' I said. 'I keep feeling a draught running across this room. Sod original windows, this place needs double glazing! I don't care what Karen says.'

'I agree,' replied Jill.

It wasn't long before we were dressed in swimming costumes and the beauty parade began. We gingerly made our way out into the garden, carefully carrying our margaritas complete with all the trimmings.

*Whoosh!* The umbrellas and sparklers disappeared. A tremendous gust of wind rushed out as soon as the back door was opened. It was as if the house had depressurised.

Suddenly I was being questioned.

'Julia, apart from being very drunk, why are you walking like that?' laughed Jill.

'If you must know, I've got a rash. Roy put flypaper in the cupboard under the sink. I didn't have my glasses on and mistook them for waxing strips. He's creating bloody man drawers all over the house!'

The laughter that followed must've carried right down the hill into the village. Though I enjoyed making and fetching drinks, my main role was to be the entertainer.

The hot tub bubbled, the drinks fizzed, the laughter didn't stop and the drinking continued into the night. We knew our antics were foolish. After all, most of us had seen the repercussions first-hand whilst working the dreaded night shift in a busy, under-staffed A & E department. Alcohol, water and heat: a recipe for disaster.

We'd got away with it for years, maybe our luck was about to run out. I noticed more beady eyes, the black cat was quietly watching from the rocks above. Bats darted back and forth above us, replacing the seagulls for the night shift. The moon provided just enough light to do our figures justice.

I was enjoying myself but feeling guilty as well, my mind kept returning to what we'd been told in the pub. I was sure Amy was feeling the same as every now and then I'd catch her thinking. The others put the glazed look down to the alcohol but I knew better.

Anaesthetic to life, they say, well it certainly helped. If I'd been sober, I don't think I would've been able to laugh and carry on messing around as we did.

Rachel returned carrying another tray of drinks. The laughter was getting louder and louder as it echoed around the rocks and up the cliffside.

'Contemporaneous note-keeping,' I bleated, impersonating Matron's voice. 'That was the bane of my life,' I spluttered. 'The documentation! Having to write "vagina warm and moist" not once, not twice, but three bloody times! Then it was "Computer says no" and you had to do it all again.'

'Warm and moist! Oh, happy days!' screeched Jill spitting her drink everywhere.

I smiled as I caught Emma whispering about a new anti-wrinkle cream for balls.

'Doesn't have a hope in hell!' I said.

'Sssh! Keep it down,' Rachel kept saying.

'Now why would I want to do that?!' I retorted in far too loud a voice.

'The neighbours!' she warned.

'Oh, I thought you were dishing out sexual advice,' I laughed.

'Oh shut up!' she said, 'Or I'll start on about the pearl necklace.'

We all burst out laughing. My face flushed red and it wasn't from the gin or the heat of the water.

'Oh! The shame and the embarrassment of it!' I said in a serious voice.

I'd spent months leading up to my thirtieth wedding anniversary proudly telling friends, relatives, work colleagues and every Tom, Dick and Harry who'd listen, that Roy was giving me a pearl necklace as a present.

Well, they'd all kept straight faces. I'm sure to this day that not everyone knew what the other meaning was. Roy didn't even know, or so he said, and he'd served in the army when he first left school.

The realisation had come cruelly at the antenatal consultant clinic. After telling Mrs Smith, the consultant, she'd taken me aside and said, in the most sober and serious manner, 'Very nice Julia, but I do hope he does it in private!'

'Oh yes,' I replied. 'I expect it'll be on the hotel balcony.'

Well, she'd literally rolled up laughing. I'd never seen her laugh before let alone in such a gregarious fashion and there were patients around as well.

'Oh, what marvellous times we've had,' slurred Karen. 'The ladies!' she said in a high-pitched voice.

'There have been some near misses as well,' Liz reminded us, 'and that one this evening definitely warrants an incident form!'

She could hardly get her words out. 'Poor Amy nearly got rammed up against the wall by that huge knob.'

'Less of the poor!' Amy replied. 'It was a travesty,' she managed to say in between hiccups. She was squinting and her nose was twitching like a rabbit's so I knew she was really drunk. This was a dangerous sign and Karen had spotted it too.

'I think we'd better go in now as it's midnight,' stated Karen. 'We've all had more than enough.'

'Did you see that? Look up there at the rocks,' pointed Liz, pulling herself onto the seat of the tub. We all looked to where she was pointing.

'The bird hide!' I gasped. We all saw the red eyes this time.

'Could be a bat?' Emma said. 'Or that cat? Ooh, I'm a poet and I don't know it,' she drunkenly chanted.

'Don't be stupid!' shouted Amy. 'Bats don't have eyes, they use sonar.'

'They still have eyes,' corrected Karen before belching loudly.

'Birdwatching is sometimes done at night time.' I prattled on. 'After all, there are owls and night larks. Someone might be bat watching.'

'Well there's certainly some old bats out tonight,' said Jill.

'It's time to go in,' ordered Karen. 'Just in case it's a Peeping Tom.' The red eyes had disappeared, whoever it was knew they'd been seen this time.

We soon dried off and returned to the lounge in our PJs. Mo was already asleep on the sofa. That was her warning sign, which was harmless. The heat of the hot tub and the excess alcohol had made us all tired judging by the amount of yawning. Mo had a good excuse as she was the oldest in the group and had recently taken early retirement.

'Dance music?' offered Emma.

I could see that Emma was just getting in the party mood as she was the only one not in bedclothes, in fact, she had on her dancing dress which she brought each year. Her lively spirit meant she was always being hassled to do nurse or midwife training but she loved her job as a top-grade care assistant, enjoying the job satisfaction without the pressure. We had all agreed this year to leave her be, after all, someone like her and her role was an essential part of the team.

'It's a bit late,' Rachel replied. 'Remember we're in a semi!'

'Anyone for a Baileys?' asked Karen, dropping ice cubes into glasses.

'Yes please!' rang around the room.

Music played softly in the background. We always tried to keep noise levels low after the complaint we'd had on our very first trip. None of us took well to criticism, especially Karen who had been horrified as the booking had been in her name.

Amy was on the floor snoring loudly with a cushion under her head.

'Time to call it a night by the looks of it,' said Rachel yawning.

'Yeah, it has been an eventful evening. Weather forecast is good for tomorrow,' Karen informed us, perking up. 'We'll go for a brisk walk before breakfast.'

I blew out the candles as we all made our way to the bedrooms. One of us was crawling. The wind chimes startled me when I reached the bottom of the stairs. I almost went to answer the door. I must've been imagining it, remembering that there were no chimes...just strings.

Amy was already asleep by the time I entered our room. We had one of the twin rooms. She'd opted for the bed by the window, mine was up against the wall. The room was spinning by the time I flopped into bed. My mind drifted into that blissful, relaxed state just before sleep takes over.

I imagined I could hear a lullaby in the distance. The most beautiful sound of an acoustic guitar softly playing a sad, lonely melody. It lulled me swiftly into a restful slumber.

It was the scream that woke me.

For a terrifying moment, I thought I was back on the labour ward. I didn't think I'd been asleep long. I felt woozy. My mouth was dry and my head was thumping. I instinctively rushed to where the scream had come from. The bathroom. The moonlight led me across the landing.

Emma was sitting on the toilet shaking, 'Oh my God! It's massive!' she cried.

I'd witnessed this scenario many times before. The sheer look of terror, that wildness in the eyes, the shaking, the clammy skin, hysteria. The pure hatred that formed the words that were spat, usually at the husband. My tutor's words rang in my ears from all those years ago. 'You will know. There will be no need for an examination. It's a madness!'

'Are you fully dilated, Emma?' I laughed. Although, I knew that you should never, ever laugh if you suspected such a thing.

Childbirth is one of the most wonderful experiences a woman can have but also probably the most painful. I had been privileged enough to both experience and witness it. The latter hundreds of times. Full dilation is a crossroads in labour, near but so far away, no wonder it induced such crazy behaviour in some women.

There was no laughter from Emma. She was terrified.

'Don't just stand there!' she shouted. 'It's behind you!'

I pulled on the light switch as she raced, sobbing, from the room. There was nothing there.

'It was a massive spider,' she was telling Mo who was now half-awake but still in her bed. Mo immediately sat bolt upright when Emma's words hit home. She was pale and her hair was matted. She normally had such beautiful hair and prided herself on it. I turned away, hoping she wouldn't look in the mirror. A shagger's crown came to mind.

Emma was a gibbering wreck.

'Nothing like a fright to sober you up!' I said feebly, trying to make the best of a bad situation.

'That spider was huge! Seriously, it wasn't a house spider. Its body was the size of a walnut and it had long legs like a spider crab. No word of a lie! I know it was big. I'm short-sighted; I wouldn't have seen it without my glasses, especially in dim light. It ran behind the sink when you put the light on. Honestly!'

'Drink some water,' I advised. We'd all had far too much alcohol which was customary on the first night but it was a feeble excuse.

I headed back to my room. The cold air on the landing made me shiver and goosebumps appeared like a rash up my arms. Could our breath create all this haze? It hung in the air like dust motes, illuminated by the moonlight. Alcoholic mist, now there's an idea I laughed to myself. Maybe it was the fog creeping in from outside.

As I passed the top of the stairs, I noticed what looked like a large stain on the carpet runner at the bottom of the stairs. Shit! Who spilt red wine?

I froze. The noise made my heart race. The wind must be playing tricks, distorting the sound, I reasoned, as it sounded just like Cheyne-Stokes breathing.

The death rattle.

It came again, this time less convincingly.

After taking a moment to gather my thoughts, I sighed with relief before reassuring myself that it was merely the sound of snoring. Poor Jill, it was much worse than last year. I hurried back to bed and literally dived under the covers. Over-indulging and mixing drinks, when would I ever learn? I cursed myself and the others as I drifted off to sleep.

It was dawn when I next opened my eyes. The room was now a dappled grey. A beam of sunlight sneaked through the gap in the curtains like a searchlight probing the room. The birdsong sounded outside with the rush of the sea in the background. The high-pitched squawk of the gulls sounded in between, breaking the symphony apart. I dozed, perfectly relaxed, the drama of the night before like a forgotten dream.

A weird sound intruded, so out of place in the harmony that was soothing me. The scratching, scraping sound was loud and sharp then it stopped abruptly. But it was the intermittent creaking and the unmistakable sound of footsteps that drew my eyes to the ceiling. However, fatigue ensured that sleep was undeterred and it whisked me away from my curiosity.

I was woken much later by the warm sunlight filling the room. The whole house was buzzing with life as if energised by solar power. Amy appeared at the door with a much-welcome cup of tea.

'Karen's not happy! There was a mouse on the table eating her cookies. I think she's right, this house is dirty,' she sighed.

I made my way downstairs. No sign of a wine stain provoked a sigh of relief as I felt for damp with my foot at the bottom of the stairs. It must've been a shadow, thank goodness. The icy-cold floor, however, was teeming with woodlice and the smell that still lingered made me retch. It was revolting. Thankfully the bustling sound of early morning conversation captured my attention, drawing me away from my grim circumstance.

Breakfast preparation was in full swing. The kitchen was like a busy café, warm and welcoming, filled with sunlight. Such a contrast to the hallway. There were smiles all around. The view from the window chased the headaches far away.

Cloudless blue sky. The sea like an aquamarine pool bathed in sunlight. The scene would make for a picture-perfect postcard.

We sat around the table, mugs in hand, waiting to see who would be the bravest and broach the subject of the ridiculous amount of alcohol we'd consumed the night before. As if on cue, Karen spoke.

'I don't need any paracetamol,' she said glaring at the packet someone had gingerly placed in the middle of the table. We all knew she had a high pain threshold and was always the first to deny any overindulgence, whether it be cake, butter or red wine. Amy nudged me under the table and Mo averted her eyes.

'I don't know about you lot,' she continued, 'but I actually didn't have a lot to drink.' Never mind the menopause, she's definitely in denial. I kept my mouth shut but someone else was braver.

'Really?!' said Jill, producing an empty bottle of Karen's favourite red wine.

'We're gonna need a bigger recycling crate,' stated Rachel pointing to the box in the corner that was already overflowing with bottles and cans.

Then it started. The worried faces, some more anxious than others. Everyone waiting to see if someone would remind them of what they'd said or done or, worse still, not remembered at all.

'Well, we all had far too much,' I chastised, looking at Emma. 'Didn't anyone hear the scream in the middle of the night?'

'What scream?' they all said together.

'See! You must've been out for the count,' I laughed. If she remembered, Emma didn't mention the spider. After all, that would've freaked everyone out.

'Jill, you sounded comatosed! Your snoring carried right up the stairs.'

'I didn't sleep down there. It was far too cold,' she replied. That's odd, I pondered, but my memory was patchy, not surprising judging by the amount of gin left in the bottle.

'We always go over the top on the first night,' Liz said reassuringly as if it was a good thing. 'It's the start of our holiday, after all.'

She was right, the party atmosphere that our get-together induced meant a foolish first-night binge was customary.

'Well, I'm gonna be good tonight,' stated Amy with her legs crossed under the table. We all nodded, knowing she only told little white lies.

Mo was reaching for the paracetamol looking very sheepish.

'Don't worry,' said Emma. 'You only fell asleep this year.'

We knew one another so well now that it was easy to notice if someone was vulnerable or stressed and liable to succumb to the often negative effects of alcohol. Watching and helping each other, ensuring that no one would come to any harm, was always a priority. We followed a code that we used to avert catastrophe when stress complicated matters.

The code phrase was 'stretch and sweep'. Those three little words were ingrained in our brains as they took up a lot of space in the antenatal clinic diary, hence they would never be forgotten. They were also easy words for any of us to drop casually into a conversation as a prompt that a situation was arising and preventative action may be required.

If the code words were given it was taken seriously and we played our parts.

Firstly, we would discreetly water down drinks with lemonade or tonic water.

Secondly, everyone would be given a large glass of iced water with a spiel about how good it is for preventing wrinkles and cystitis.

Thirdly, the culprit would be plied with garlic bread and nibbles to soak up the booze. The latter was always the easiest option.

If further action was necessary, it would be the drastic action of stretch and sweep, which only took place in extreme circumstances as it involved literally stretching over and sweeping up all the glasses so the alcohol could be quickly thrown down the sink. This was only done as a last resort as it was indiscriminate, and to throw alcohol away went against our ethos of waste not, want not!

'What did we win on the scratch cards?' asked Mo. Christ, I didn't remember doing them.

'Fuck all,' answered Rachel.

'Just before I dropped off to sleep I thought I heard someone playing the guitar,' Liz said. No one answered and she didn't push it further. It must've been the next-door neighbour, I reasoned.

'Who's coming for a brisk walk along the coastal path?' questioned Karen standing to attention. 'That'll clear our heads.'

We all looked at each other knowingly - she has got a headache! Minutes later she was poised at the door in full hiking kit, trekking poles and all. I knew, like me, they'd all laugh when her back was turned so I rushed upstairs to get ready.

My head was throbbing just like it was that Saturday morning ten years ago back where it all began...

# CHAPTER 4
*The Motorhome 2009*

We were staying on a campsite. Our accommodation back then was Karen's motorhome and a two-man tent. We had all woken up with hangovers having gone overboard on the first night. I was feeling terrible, not just hungover, so I stayed in the motorhome while they went to the beach. My head was thumping but it was the vomiting that made it impossible for me to venture outside. I blamed Amy's chicken kebabs as I had only had a few glasses of scrumpy. Oh, and some wine. In all honesty, I was glad to be alone as I was embarrassed and ashamed. I tortured myself with a rerun of the events of the night before. Well, the parts that I could remember.

We had intended to hire a beach hut and a picnic lunch was planned. I was to phone them when I felt up to joining them. Unfortunately, the phone call would be made sooner than anticipated and the day, well, the weekend, would be brutally cut short.

I jumped up, startled by the ferocious knocking on the door. There was a diesel engine choking in the background, the fumes crept in the window worsening my nausea. The angry muttering and swearing alongside the constant rap on the door told me that this was an unwelcome visitor who was not going away. I realised too late that the door wasn't locked and in an instant, it was forcefully yanked open and my suspicions were confirmed. It was the campsite owner.

My fragile state and the sight of the vomit bowl fueled his anger, his actions were now justified and he relished the fact as a smile formed amidst the grimace. A lanky teenager lurked in the background looking more embarrassed than I was.

His words were forceful and straight to the point, to interrupt would have been futile. We were to leave the campsite by 12 noon at the latest or he would tow us off. We had been there less than 24 hours. This was a disaster. Our first trip away ruined, cut short and it was all my fault. Well, mostly.

Meanwhile, the nosey parkers had gathered like a cult. Dog walkers, families, couples taking a morning stroll. They were all eager to see what all the commotion was about. Well, they knew. After all, there had been a lot of complaints or so he'd said.

The sound of tent zips buzzed in the background as heads bobbed in and out. I could sense eyes and ears all directed at our motorhome with utter disdain. A blind shot up unexpectedly in the motorhome alongside, startling them and me. It revealed an old couple glued to the window listening. My face flushed a deeper hue as I recognised the man. He had provided a flannel as I'd streaked from the shower block late the night before.

I was perturbed as the whole fiasco was petty really. There had been no loud music. Apparently, it was the laughter that had carried across the campsite that kept people awake. Our motorhome had acted like a giant microphone. Emma and I heard the farts from the tent!

I made the call as soon as he had gone. It was short and sweet. 'You need to come back!' I gasped, almost in tears. They had only just parked the car.

It wasn't long before I heard the car return. They rushed in like a gaggle of geese, all talking at the same time. Only Karen was quiet. I knew she was worried as it was her name on the booking form.

'What did he say?' demanded Amy. I could see she was fuming. Before I had finished telling them what had happened, she was halfway out the door with Rachel and Mo hot on her heels. I knew they were heading to the reception.

I noticed the couple next door had conveniently moved their table and chairs nearer to our motorhome, ensuring that they were in earshot. They both looked away as we rushed out the door. They each had a sausage dog nestled on their laps. There was no frenzied yapping this morning. Mouths were clamped shut. They didn't want to miss a thing. This was exciting stuff for a quiet campsite.

'Oh God!' sighed Karen, shaking her head in despair as she saw Amy marching across the field.

'Come on,' said Jill. She was calm and collected as usual. The perfect peacekeeper. Her skills would be needed by the looks of it.

As it turned out, he was all mouth and no trousers. He must have caught sight of us trooping across the grass and didn't fancy his chances. The reception block was raised, providing a panoramic view of the whole site. We saw him exit, climb aboard the tractor and hastily retreat. He was in such a hurry that he ran over the egg delivery which ignited Amy's anger further.

'What a waste,' sighed Karen.

Karen and Amy went inside to speak to the middle-aged woman behind the desk. There had been a few complaints apparently from regular visitors who were classed as VIPs. His wife reiterated what he had told me. Her face winced like she'd just sucked a lemon when she added that the group of men had also been asked to leave. 'We will not be accepting all male or all female groups in the future,' she said curtly, ending the conversation.

We strode back feeling defeated and that was a feeling that didn't come easily as it was unfamiliar. More pressingly, we needed to decide what to tell our families as they would definitely want to know why we were back a day early.

'Let's try and enjoy the rest of the day,' said Rachel despondently.

'How about a picnic lunch before we go home?' suggested Karen. 'There's a huge grass car park overlooking the beach. The views are stunning!'

We all agreed that was a fantastic idea. We found a lovely spot. The car park was massive and quite empty, most people preferred to park nearer the beach. The view was spectacular, as promised.

Clear, blue sky enveloped us and the sun blazed up above. Rays of sunlight doused our faces warming us through. A yellow sheen reflected from the hundreds of buttercups and tinted our skin. Karen looked almost golden.

'She looks jaundiced,' laughed Amy. 'Too much butter!'

The lush grass, scattered with daisies and purple clover, ran down to the cliff edge to merge with the sea. The grass had grown long behind us and naturally formed a wildflower meadow bordering the car park, providing a rainbow of colour all around.

Karen laid down the tartan picnic blankets and we arranged the few chairs and the camping table. Perfect.

Well, almost.

Mo nudged me and pointed out the familiar motorhome that was trundling uphill towards us. It was the nosy old couple and the dachshunds that had been parked next to us at the campsite.

'Damn!' cursed Karen. She had noticed as well.

'Are they following us?' murmured Jill.

Unfortunately, the motorhome was being reversed alongside us. The engine spluttered and diesel fumes wafted towards us.

'That exhaust looks knackered,' remarked Rachel, choking as she spoke.

The woman was now directing from behind the van as he reversed into position. 'They couldn't have got any closer,' moaned Amy and she was right. There was practically an entire car park to choose from.

Amy was taken in by the woman's signalling. I was taken in by the fact that the motorhome was still reversing and getting dangerously close to a fence post. She was still flapping her hands towards her face when we heard the thump and the sound of smashing glass. He had reversed into the post. The door slammed and the swearing began. The dachshunds were frenzied.

'I was swatting a bee away,' she shouted. 'You idiot!'

I was feeling better. The bout of laughter, as always, had chased my worries away. The fresh sea air which was blowing up the hill was invigorating.

'Look at all this red sand on the motorhome,' said Karen. 'How strange.'

Seagulls soared above the ocean and buzzards patrolled the airways above us. They floated up and down effortlessly on the thermals, always looking for prey. There was plenty here. Rabbits ventured from the long grass, furtively keeping to the edges. The sky was dotted with bright colours as kites billowed back and forth above, delighting the smiling faces that peered upwards.

'I'm starving,' announced Emma suddenly.

It wasn't long before a delectable picnic was laid out before us. We certainly knew how to make the best of a bad situation. We were used to doing that daily at work. It was ingrained in our psyche.

Karen was mumbling inside the motorhome. 'There's ginger beer in the fridge - non-alcoholic, of course - and lemonade.'

Liz helped her with the bottles which were nicely chilled.

'Good little fridge,' praised Amy. 'I'll use up that leftover wine,' she added, grabbing the chardonnay. Things were looking up.

'Hair of the dog?' she asked.

'No thanks!' I said, and I meant it. I was sticking to water and food.

It looked scrumptious. The picnic had undoubtedly inspired our cold fayre tradition which was an essential we now enjoyed on every trip. There was crusty bread which Karen had buttered, thickly. Homemade strawberry jam or paté for spreading. An array of cheeses took centre stage with homemade chutney, pickled onions, cherry tomatoes and grapes. Ham on the bone, pork pies, hard-boiled eggs and cocktail sausages completed the line-up. It was all swilled down with lashings of ginger beer and lemonade.

We just about managed to eat the last of Mo's Victoria sandwich with some clotted cream.

'It's tiring all this eating,' groaned Karen as she settled down for a nap.

We all found cushions and our own little patch of grass. It was blissful. The waves were soothing in the distance and the birdsong around us was gentle. The row had ended next door.

I think we all dozed off in minutes.

We had a serious group discussion mid-afternoon. We couldn't decide what we would tell our families, a toned-down version of the truth most likely. However, we did decide to make a weekend break an annual event.

We'd had lots of laughs and bonded well. We knew our friendships were something special. The excitement came buzzing back and I was soon my old self. I couldn't sit still and neither could Amy.

'We need a name for our gang,' I mumbled as I paced crazily around them. The response was lukewarm so Amy changed the subject.

'Please don't ever mention the grass. It was embarrassing.'

'No need to. We don't really know for sure that that's what it was,' replied Mo.

'Burning it, I mean!' interjected Amy. 'The barbecue!' she said slowly. 'He complained about the burnt patch of grass, you know.'

'Smoking weed, I never would have envisioned that,' added Liz.

'Well, it certainly wasn't intentional, if that's what it was,' said Karen.

I sat quietly now, a passive observer of the conversation. Some of the events had been out of our control but it had still resulted in us being thrown off the site. We needed to be careful, there was a code of conduct to adhere to even out of uniform.

'It was those men,' whispered Emma, still looking at the ground.

I didn't look up, I daren't.

'Well, it's all in the past now,' stated Karen, dusting off the crumbs from her top.

'Yes, it's no good raking over shit,' Rachel added. 'We'll lay down some rules and start afresh, ready for next year. Learn from our mistakes.'

I really hoped there would be a next year. I sensed Mo's eyes on me and glanced sideways. She was smiling and so were the others.

'Good idea, Julia. We do need a name for the group,' she said.

So that's what we did next. After a bit more banter and quite a few laughs, we came up with a name. And on the serious side, we made a pact. What happened on this trip would never be mentioned. It was our secret.

It paled in comparison to what would happen ten years later on our anniversary trip.

# CHAPTER 5

I stopped reminiscing and rushed downstairs to join them. It was just three of us for the walk and if we timed it right we'd be back just in time for breakfast.

I knew from experience that it would be a fast walk, more like a race. It was sure to be a competition between Karen and Amy as to who could go the fastest. Their rivalry was potent and meant that even walking became a serious contest. Karen's new trekking poles were hampering her style. I noticed her gait was awkward and out of time, Amy had noticed too and had taken full advantage of it to quickly take the lead. She looked ridiculous, by the looks of it she'd been watching those walking races on TV.

It was a beautiful morning, glorious sun and clear blue sky. The grass glistened with dewdrops, daisies scattered in between like confetti, and the wind was now a gentle, warm breeze. We had to go through the churchyard to get to the coastal path and I knew Amy would love this route as churches and graveyards were amongst her favourite places. She came to an abrupt halt halfway down the graveyard path, narrowly missing being speared up the backside by a hiking pole.

'For God's sake!' Karen cursed before seeing her advantage and racing on ahead.

Amy was standing very still, mesmerised, maybe remembering past romantic liaisons. Or maybe not, as she wasn't smiling, quite the opposite, she looked glum. As I got closer, I could see she was reading the engraving on a headstone with great concentration. She certainly did look miserable so I gave her a few minutes of peace before my audacious outburst.

'Hence loathed melancholy,' I chanted crazily, manically waving my hands in front of her face. She ignored me initially then pointed at the words that had unsettled her.

'Beloved son, tragically taken aged 44 years.' There was a guitar and music notes etched into the granite.

'It must be the chap the barmaid told us about,' she said with sadness. The solemn atmosphere was broken quite rudely by Karen and the rooks as they circled above. The crows' raspy caws were impudent as if we were trespassing, and Karen's instruction was brash.

'Get a move on you two!' she shouted. 'You're hampering my rhythm.'

'And your style, I hope,' Amy replied quietly.

The crisp morning air and hunger pangs, judging by the noise from her stomach, made her snap from her pensiveness with renewed vigour and she soon caught Karen up. Her tight lycra cycling shorts were almost as bad as leggings and it looked as if she'd mistakenly left the seat pad in. Unless, of course, she'd succumbed to Tena Lady.

Let them battle. I kept my distance, determined to relax and take in the scenery as my headache had gone.

The path weaved between yellow gorse and ferns, like a lazy meandering stream taking me on a journey. Rocks broke up the colours, jutting out like giant molars pushed up from the earth. I could hear the sheep munching on the grass as they began their laborious day of grazing. Avoiding the rabbit holes took some skill, at least we all had our walking boots on. It was peaceful and relaxing. A perfect start to the day.

They wouldn't be chatting, I knew they'd both be conserving energy for the home straight when Amy would most definitely take the lead.

The air was still, no noisy gale like yesterday, what a contrast. I noticed a cormorant perched on a rocky outcrop below, poised, enchanted by the turquoise water hiding its quarry. So still like a statue, it waited, knowing from experience the precise moment when its dive would guarantee the silver prize it craved.

Every now and then the ring of the oystercatchers would sound across the sky. I was suddenly overcome with nostalgia for past family holidays. It reminded me of the guitar music I'd heard the night before. Liz had mentioned it this morning. It must've been the next-door neighbour.

We rounded the headland and we were soon heading back. My breathing deepened and my legs ached, all uphill now, unfortunately. I was starving. The thought of breakfast spurred me on as I'm sure it did the others.

We were blasted by a strong gust of cold air as we opened the front door.

'Windy Passage, my ass,' cussed Amy. 'This hallway is weird and that smell is disgusting,' she choked, holding her nose.

'We'll get some air freshener and this will go in the review. Don't you worry,' chortled Karen hardly able to conceal her excitement. There must be a problem with the Victorian pipework. There was probably no mains drainage.

We'd done well, perfect timing. Breakfast smelt delicious and was about to be served. I eyed up Mo's fried eggs and made the rash decision to be veggie and not vegan, for today anyhow. Surely one free-range egg was justified after the walk I'd done and, after all, I wouldn't be having any crispy bacon or sausages.

It was a full English fry-up of mega proportions and cooked to perfection as usual. The room was silent as it always was when we were eating. Until, of course, someone needed a breather or had something important to say, or perhaps had a question to ask or was looking to start an argument.

'You're still veggie then, Ju?' quizzed Mo in a dubious tone.

'Oh yes, of course,' I answered sincerely. 'But I do eat fish.' My ignorance was blatant, laid bare to tempt any inquisitive or argumentative minds. The remark was ignored as brain cells were otherwise occupied. It was taxing deciding what ketchup you wanted and it was rude to speak with a full mouth. And all mouths here were well and truly full.

'Right! Let's get organised! We need a plan,' suggested Rachel after we'd finished eating. 'What about the beach this morning and shopping after lunch?'

'Lunch,' Amy screeched at the top of her voice. 'After all you've just eaten?!' she sneered.

'Well, I fancy a pasty for lunch,' dared Liz, burping as she leaned back to loosen her belt.

'Or one of those freshly-made, crusty baguettes from that little bakery, remember?' asked Emma, goading Amy.

'Fish and chips would be nice,' added Jill.

Amy left the table in disgust, tutting and patting her stomach. 'They wonder why they're bloated,' I heard her cursing under her breath. Minutes later she returned looking positively sheepish. 'Anyone for a coffee?' she asked politely, a peace offering for her outburst. She looked like she had a seat pad at the front of her cycle shorts now.

'Spanish lessons going ok?' I asked Karen. My supposedly innocent question immediately sent a vision of my hand stirring a huge wooden spoon. We needed to let our breakfast settle and an argument was a good way to get the digestive juices flowing.

'Waste of time and money,' piped up Amy plonking the coffees on the table. 'You'll never learn at our age. It's like driving lessons. The older you are the harder it gets and you're less likely to pass the test,' she stated, looking down her nose at Emma.

She's in an argumentative mood, I thought, and I knew Karen thought the same as her posture had changed. She'd even rolled up her sleeves! She was ready to pounce and she did.

'Oh and I suppose you think sign language is an effective way of communicating in a foreign country then, Amy?'

You could almost hear the click as Amy pulled her neck in. Amy would never admit defeat, it was one of her faults, even if she knew she was wrong. Sheer bloody-mindedness. Those two were more alike than they would ever care to admit, we all knew that.

I knew we were all remembering that weekend in Spain and, judging by our facial expressions, were trying not to laugh.

It had been four of us on a weekend trip to Karen's holiday apartment. We'd had a great evening, a delicious meal and a few drinks in an authentic tapas bar by the harbour. We were enjoying a stroll home along the promenade. It was after midnight and there were lots of Spanish families still picnicking on the beach in the moonlight. Such a lovely tradition. We'd almost got back without incident, after all, we'd drunk plenty of wine and sangria, but then she saw them. Bloody fishermen!

Mo and I had sighed and sat on the wall alongside the prom, knowing it was futile to try and stop her. Karen walked home. We weren't far and she must have sensed the oncoming palaver and was having none of it.

I can see it now, Amy marching down the beach. She stumbled a few times but never lost a shoe, handbag, or her nerve. The old Spanish men must've been so relaxed on their deckchairs, blankets over legs, rods in hand, quietly waiting for the fish of the night to bite. They were the older generation, great grandfathers most likely. It was not a tourist area but a quiet, traditional working seaside town, that's what we all liked about it. Of course, they didn't speak English, and why would they, so she used sign language to communicate.

We could see it quite clearly as she was lit up by the moon and the street lamp. There she stood in her pretty sundress pointing to her wedding ring, then with thumb and index finger she started rubbing it up and down. The more they didn't understand, the more vigorously she rubbed. All she was trying to say was that her husband was a fisherman.

It wasn't long before they both jumped up, throwing their blankets aside, forgetting their fish, sending buckets of worms flying everywhere. For old men, they moved swiftly. We'd rescued her, of course, in hysterics.

She'd obviously not learned the error of her ways...or she'd forgotten.

Karen had left the table in disgust and was chopping various types of mushrooms for the stroganoff we would be having for supper. 'It's all in the preparation,' she was mumbling, along with various obscenities.

It wasn't long before we were setting off for the beach.

As we were driving away, I noticed the next-door neighbour closing her door. It was the barmaid we'd spoken to the night before. Strange she didn't mention where she lived considering what she had told us. I suppose it made more sense as to how she knew all the gory details.

She would definitely have been interviewed by the police. Nosy neighbours provide lots of witness statements, that's for sure. Nevertheless, a bit fishy.

A five-minute downhill drive took us to one of the most spectacular beaches in the area. When the weather was good, like today, it could outshine most beaches abroad. The sheer expanse of golden sand backed by windswept dunes and huge rolling, white-tipped waves domineering the horizon made for an awe-inspiring view. The magnitude of the beach and the fact that it never got crowded added to its splendour. It was always breezy and the strong winds off the Atlantic produced some of the best surfing waves in the country.

We'd surfed one year, or at least tried to. Karen had insisted, dishing out wetsuits she'd hired for us all. The waves had subsided by the time we had squeezed them on. It was like trying to pull on a giant anti-embolism stocking. A beach hut had been booked but didn't get used as the beach had been evacuated due to a bomb scare. At least the surfing got cut short, we'd agreed with relief. It took us ages to peel the wet suits off. We were the last off the beach.

Liz found a sheltered spot and we spread out our towels. No bikinis now, just shorts and cami tops, and no leggings either, they'd been banned after the first year.

'Where're your leggings, Amy?' teased Jill. Amy played along mimicking her actions from all those years ago. We were sitting in just about the same place as we had back then. Amy moved a short distance away and lay down on her back with her mouth open and we all laughed at the memory.

On that particular occasion, she'd worn the tightest leggings she owned and the shortest top. She'd basked in the sun oblivious to the unwanted attention from the old man and his dog nearby. The more he'd edged his towel nearer, the louder they'd laughed. I had failed to see what was so funny. They kept sniggering and whispering. Eventually, I picked out the words 'camel toe'.

My eyes were drawn straight to her feet which were petite and perfectly formed, nails manicured and painted. Camels' feet were ugly, I'd thought. In my naivety, I said aloud, 'What's wrong? She's got beautiful feet.'

Jill's laughing had sounded like a donkey and Amy nearly choked to death.

'We mustn't forget to buy some air freshener. That smell in the hallway is getting worse,' Liz said as she dished out water bottles and suncream. 'I think we need to investigate where it's coming from. I'm convinced it's not the drains, in fact, it smells like rotting flesh.'

'You're right,' both Karen and I said in unison. We had all cared for patients with wound infections during our careers. The odour is never forgotten. That unmistakable stench could lead you straight to the source when you walked onto the ward.

'The hallway is always icy cold,' commented Emma. She was straight-faced and serious, quite the contrary to Karen who decided to lighten the mood.

'How exciting! A haunted house!' she blurted out in a voice two octaves higher than usual. Meanwhile, I glanced at Amy. She was deep in thought biting her nails.

The nervous energy petered out as the morning went by and worries were cast aside for the time being. We lazed on the sand dozing until a stomach rumbled just like an alarm clock.

'What about ice creams instead of lunch?' Mo suggested. A brilliant idea, we all agreed.

Ice creams purchased, Emma devoured her cone whilst telling me a rude story about being caught by her mother. Jill was eavesdropping and piped up, 'You got off lightly girl! In my day, you got a hiding for sucking your thumb, never mind anything else!'

Laughter filled the air again. That was what we loved the most about our weekends away. As I lazed in the sun, memories from my career in the NHS came flooding back bringing smiles to my sun-drenched face...

Seeing the funny side of things had definitely helped me along life's journey, particularly where work was concerned. It helped others as well, I'd seen it from experience many times. You had a far better shift if everyone was happy. Of course, in my line of work that wasn't always possible.

There were times when there could never be laughter, just sadness. But fate had been kind and the happier times far outweighed those dark days. I knew I'd been privileged. My career had allowed me to share the most intimate moments of life. The joyous, euphoric beginning and the finality of the journey's end. I had been lucky as the final few hours, followed by the release from this earth, that I'd witnessed first-hand had always been peaceful.

A cloud crept over the sun and chilled my skin making me feel uneasy. Doubt wormed its way back again when I thought about my predicament. Had I really jacked it all in over a shit day in the clinic? Now I was jobless. Well, apart from the agency work. 'On impulse' was an understatement.

The final straw had been that awful day in the clinic and a series of unfortunate events leading to my resignation. Not having my reading glasses had been the catalyst. Several minor misdemeanours later, I went to the waiting room to call a patient through for her appointment. It was the part of the clinic that I hated. The room was usually packed with miserable faces, often understandably so as appointments frequently ran behind time.

'April,' I called to no avail. Faces were getting redder and angrier by the minute as it wasn't their name being called and the consultant was irritated as the conveyor belt stalled.

'April Cottage,' I said louder but still no response. I turned to get another set of notes and heard laughter in the room mingled with angry words. A mild-mannered lady raised her hand.

'I live in April Cottage,' she said. That day got worse. The clinic overran by a couple of hours so there was no lunch break.

The final nail in the coffin came that afternoon. The clinic continued, now run by a locum consultant. I still find it hard to believe what he actually said to that poor woman. It was a sentence with dire consequences as he never returned and neither did I, not to the clinic anyhow. He had lifted the sheet to examine her. I was the chaperone.

'I'd have brought my lawnmower if I'd known,' he said sarcastically. That was it. Shocking. Oh, he got a dressing down later from myself and Matron. My resignation letter went in the very next day. Now I certainly had more control and a better work-life balance. No on-calls, that was fantastic.

On the whole, it was a good decision.

The biggest bonus was more time to do what I'd always wanted to…like writing.

# CHAPTER 6

The afternoon brought more sunshine and more food. We'd driven a short distance to the nearest seaside town. After a brisk walk from the car park, Emma felt giddy. She blamed low blood sugar so we'd all sympathised and bought bags of chips. Proper deep-fried chips, doused in salt and vinegar and wrapped up in newspaper. Authentic, traditional and scrumptious, we all agreed as we walked down the seafront.

The promenade was splendid. The original Victorian lamps and railings retained their pomp and provided a seaside atmosphere from times past. Nostalgia was spoiled momentarily by a mob of frenzied seagulls fearlessly dive bombing us to steal our chips. They were unsuccessful as we were all highly defensive where food was concerned.

A steely-grey, rocky cliff loomed at the end of the promenade. It was indented with tunnels and caves, providing an air of drama and mystery. Mo rushed ahead to explore the biggest tunnel. She could hardly contain her excitement.

'It's closed off to the public!' she gabbled, pulling on the ropes as she read the notice. 'There's a wedding at 3 o'clock.'

'Who wants to get married in a cave?' sighed Amy, shaking her head in disbelief.

We peered through the tunnel which led to a romantic pebbled cove on the other side which was all set up for the wedding.

'Oh, it's beautiful,' cooed Liz. 'How romantic! What a setting and what perfect weather.'

'Right! Let's get organised,' ordered Rachel. 'We need somewhere to sit.' She need not have worried as Mo had already laid claim to the wall behind us. Wedding watching was one of our favourite past times so this was an added bonus. I was particularly enthused as I had a family wedding on the horizon and this was the perfect way to get ideas of what not to wear.

We were experts at this as we had done it many times before. Amy did a quick scout of the area to judge where cars would be parked and what direction the guests would come from. We were in luck, the wall was in a prime position. By the looks of it, guests would come down a steep path, adding to the excitement as Karen surmised it would be difficult to navigate in high-heeled shoes.

Jill noted the brisk breeze. 'Hats and skirts will be a challenge,' she said with glee. Not that any of us wanted it spoiled, of course. It was just a bit of fun and that's what our breaks were all about.

Mo was sat on the end thus being the first to spot them. She was a classy dresser so we allowed her to make the first comment or start the nudging which would follow down the line. She was so excited, tapping her feet and checking her watch.

'Calm down!' I laughed. 'It's nearly time.'

'It'll be the groom and best man first,' she jittered, her whole body quivering. Thank goodness she was there or we would never have guessed.

Amy had no patience and stood up like a meerkat, ready to signal us. 'They're here,' she shouted rushing to her seat.

'Quiet,' urged Karen, 'and no laughing'.

'Or crying!' I added, looking at Emma.

The groom and best man arrived first, Mo nodded her head in triumph as if she'd won a Nobel Prize. They lingered around the entrance to welcome people, nervously laughing and chatting.

'No complaints there,' sighed Liz winking and we all agreed.

Part of the fun was guessing who the guests were. Spotting the mother of the bride was ranked the highest, mother of the groom came a close second. The next best achievement was pairing couples, especially of the same sex. Observing an argument was coveted by all, as was an affair. I think we all secretly wondered if we'd ever witness what Emma had seen all those years ago on the bonnet of a car. It was never mentioned, not even after a few drinks. We'd all been sworn to silence besides it was too embarrassing, especially as it was someone else's husband.

The excitement was building as the wedding cars arrived along with the crowds. Amy was itching to see how the bride would arrive, hoping for a horse and cart I suspected. A steady stream of guests made their way down the slope. The atmosphere was buzzing and the smiles and laughter were infectious.

We oohed and aahed and there was a certain amount of finger-pointing and elbow-digging. I'm sure Mo could get a job as a ventriloquist if she ever needed to work again. To be honest, on the whole, the outfits were stunning. Everything was going smoothly. We sat chatting amongst ourselves, well, not Mo, she remained on the lookout.

I suddenly felt her grab my knee and heard her snigger. Here we go again! I took a deep breath and willed myself not to laugh as I knew this was the signal. I nudged Amy and the nudging rippled down the line. Of course, by now we'd all seen what Mo had seen and we were desperately trying to control ourselves.

'Stop it!' Karen chirped in a high-pitched, quivering voice.

'Oh no! How gaudy! Bright red, canary yellow and royal blue. Here's what not to wear,' Mo whispered under her breath.

'Actually, I like the red hat and the shoes,' said Jill. 'Amy, that's your style of shoe,' she tittered, smirking at the kitten-heeled, red patent shoes adorned with a huge gold buckle.

'Not my style at all,' piped up Karen. Clearly. I looked down at her flat, brown lace-ups. 'They are so comfortable,' she muttered for the hundredth time as she tucked her feet in.

'I just don't get the royal blue belt,' grumbled Mo with utter disappointment.

'The big, gold buckle on the belt matches the big, gold buckle on her shoes which I love,' declared Amy.

'Well, she certainly stands out from the crowd,' Liz commented. 'It's unusual...high-end designer, for sure.'

The dress was canary yellow, high-waisted with a flared skirt. She was a curvy woman, at least size 16 I judged. Big boobs and ass, an hourglass figure, just what I always coveted.

She continued her descent quite elegantly but about halfway down disaster struck. A strong gust of wind blew her dress up around her ears and whisked off her hat. Her husband caught the hat quite expertly whilst the wedding photographer snapped her Brazilian!

'Oh my God! Red hat, no knickers!' screeched Emma in disbelief. We managed to stop laughing by the time she passed us.

'There you go, Mo,' said Rachel. 'Blue belt solved. It matches her eyeshadow.'

She was a pretty woman, we all agreed as she greeted her son. None of us had noticed the mother of the bride, which wasn't necessarily a good thing.

'Better to be noticed, than to not be noticed at all,' mumbled Amy dubiously as they all made their way through the tunnel.

Mo stood up. She was near frantic now as the bride was arriving. She, too, had to run the gauntlet down the slope. The wind seemed to drop, out of courtesy perhaps, as she made it down unscathed and smiling. She looked stunning as they always do, an aura of happiness surrounded her, radiating out and infecting us and those nearby.

We edged closer wanting to see the dress more closely. That was the prize. It was a beauty and we knew Mo would describe it in great detail later.

It was the palest ivory, almost white. The sleeves were long and sheer. The fitted bodice bound in a delicate lace revealed the amplest bosom. The skirt was free-flowing from the waist down and so sheer it mimicked the morning mist. Her veil was long and finer still, like tissue paper, almost too delicate to touch. It was edged with the lace of the bodice. Absolutely beautiful!

The bridesmaids wore royal blue, the subtle shimmer told of silk. Mo was nodding her head and smiling in approval.

'What a fabulous day we've had!' said a teary-eyed Emma.

We arrived back at the house late afternoon and, coincidentally, our neighbour, the infamous barmaid, had also returned at the same time. Was it a coincidence?

'Hi there,' called Amy.

She had seen us, I was sure, but she avoided eye contact and didn't answer. She peered nervously towards the upstairs window before rushing into the house.

'How odd!' I said. 'We couldn't get a word in edgeways the other night when she was telling us that story.'

'What story?' asked Rachel. We didn't answer and she didn't push it further.

'Well she was at work and getting paid, surprising how people's characters change outside the workplace,' Amy whispered to me.

I'd seen that forlorn, beaten-down look before. I had a sneaking suspicion that something wasn't right as I followed them into the house, which itself seemed to beckon me indoors.

# CHAPTER 7
## 'Sue'

She almost slammed the door. Her nerves were definitely getting the better of her, which wasn't surprising all things considered. Inside she froze, willing the door to prop her up. The sigh of relief came but her heart was still thumping.

She'd told herself not to get involved but that was easier said than done. What she had been roped into went against her very nature and it was even harder this time as they seemed so nice, living life to the full by the looks of it. Something she had never done. Never had the chance. Well, you make your own bed!

'Please no self-pity or excuses,' she whispered, hoping that words would prove stronger than thoughts. *Chance would be a fine thing.* She listened intently for the soothing creaks that assured her he was out of earshot. The first sign of madness, well, it was a long time coming. Thinking was safer than speaking but, unfortunately, she couldn't always control what came out of her mouth. She was stupid that's why, or so she'd been told.

'You had plenty of chances but no backbone, no ambition and no ability,' his words rang in her head, followed by those of her mother's.

'You're just a silly love-struck teenager infatuated with an older man. He's your first boyfriend!'

Those were the very words her mother had uttered and they had stuck in her head and had, unfortunately, rung true, like most of the other things her mother had said. If only she had listened. But she had learned many lessons along the way and that was something she'd put to good use.

Tentatively advising her own children had been paramount but the naive, arrogant words she had screeched at her mother had now been thrown back in her face. History repeating itself. Sometimes she thought her daughter was an actual clone of herself. Reprimanded by her mother and now her kids. Would she ever win?! All Sue could do was watch and hope they didn't make too many mistakes. When they invariably did, she'd be there to pick up the pieces. So far, so good. They were doing well. The very thought brought a smile to her face and gave her the strength to carry on.

However, the smile was short-lived as her mind wandered to a place devoid of kind thoughts...just full of regrets. These blues were getting more and more frequent and with them came more frequent 'if onlys'.

If only she had taken her parents' advice and finished the college course. She'd have been a veterinary nurse at least. There wasn't a hope in hell of a woman becoming a vet in those days unless, of course, you were from a rich family. Times were different then, a man's world most definitely.

Breathing normally now and feeling somewhat relaxed, the voice of reason soothed her. She had chosen her path, her two children were worth it all and more. She knew, if given a second chance, she would do it all again.

A loud thud startled her, breaking the chain of thought. He must be shifting stuff around up in the loft. At least he was preoccupied which gave her time to mull things over.

She slowed and deepened her breathing, calming herself with the thoughts she'd practised many times before. You've done what was asked of you so relax. There will be no fights or arguments, relax, but she couldn't relax because she knew that she hadn't done exactly what he had asked.

The most important part had been purposely left out and God help her if he ever found out.

Darren was moving about up in the loft. She could tell by the erratic movements that he was animated, high on adrenaline and those pills. Wound up and ready to execute his plan. Lord knows what he'd been up to this morning, opening parcels judging by the empty packaging strewn everywhere. Online shopping was the lesser of his addictions. He spent half his life logged on, staring at the screen like a zombie, researching, purchasing and delving into the dark web. It was shocking what a disturbed individual could purchase at the click of a button.

But it was none of her business, he was entitled to do what he liked as it was his money. After all, he had a professional career with a top-rate company pension and lump sum. She would be lucky to come out with a full state pension and that wouldn't be for years. Oh, here we go again. She just couldn't stop herself. Optimism was banned. It was a precursor to disappointment. Years of brainwashing had taken its toll.

Menial jobs were all she could do. His mocking words had almost become an anthem. 'You're a dumb bitch with no education!' Time and time again he would add this to his final sentence. Never mind the fact that the house had been run and children nurtured, that counted for nothing. When she looked back on it, she had just been another trophy to add to his collection.

Thank goodness he had used some of his pension's lump sum to convert the loft. The crude attic was now a cluttered space full of gadgets he collected and hoarded, some were still unopened in boxes. Glass jars of dried herbs and fungi were lined up on shelves, but it was the little white pills and that bloody huge black spider that really sent a shiver up her spine. She had never gone up there after that arrived. The loft room was entirely his domain now and the less she knew about it the better.

Life had changed drastically for the two of them after he took early retirement. Among other things, it seemed to accentuate the age gap. He openly admitted that he felt unimportant and under-stimulated. She suspected that he was bored. In her eyes, boredom was the root of the problem, most definitely, though he would never admit it.

They'd opted for a fresh start to solve the problem but moving away from family and friends at this time of life had turned out to be a big mistake, especially for her. The isolation, loss and regret was soul-destroying. The fact that he wouldn't support her had turned out to be a bonus. She had found herself a job and maintained her independence and she had actually found happiness, eventually. Time away from the nightmare existence at home was the only thing keeping her alive. A tentative smile graced her for a short while.

The tea in the mug was cold by now, like her feelings towards him. The mirror caught her reflection unawares. They weren't laughter lines, they were wrinkles and for some reason that made her smile again. Can a smile make your brain react in a certain way? She had read that somewhere. Happy memories emerged from nowhere and she stared dreamily out of the window.

The view was both relaxing and uplifting, consoling her and momentarily taking away this whole, sorry mess. The view was the main reason they'd bought the house. But no matter how beautiful, despair, worry and dread would soon seep back, taking over like a hideous vine destroying her sanity. She rolled her thumbs nervously, disgusted by the bitten-down nails. The sunlight highlighted the faded yellow bruises, thumbprints, that marked her forearms.

She need not worry for the time being. Darren's mood would be good now. The planning, preparation and excitement of executing his plan would fuel his energy, give him a high.

Why had it all gone wrong? The first few months of the 'fresh start' had been idyllic. A stunning house by the sea full of character and charm. Views to die for. They'd been happy, well, almost. It all went downhill when the man next door moved back to London and let the house out.

'Tenants. That's all we need,' he'd cursed. He had made his mind up before they even moved in.

They seemed like a nice couple, creative sorts. Musicians, it turned out. If only they'd been artists or writers. It was the noise that drove him insane, igniting his temper which she took the brunt of. It was usually verbal but there had been bad days when he had lost control, unable to manage his violent anger. Those days had left physical scars which had healed but the mental cruelty would never be forgotten.

Nevertheless, there was more to it than that. She knew deep down that it was jealousy that had triggered the path of self-destruction and led to those terrible consequences. The metallic taste of blood from her bitten lip brought reality to that horrific memory.

There had been respite after the accident but not for long. Things went from bad to worse when the holiday lets started. He should've put a bullet through his head or she should have, after all, there was a gun up in the loft. Better that he dies than anyone else.

Hindsight was a wonderful thing.

At the very least, she should have had him sectioned.

# CHAPTER 8

I opened the door and stopped dead in my tracks. The blast of cold air was ferocious, whipping our faces and watering eyes. The stench it carried was so repulsive it made us urge and that took a lot for a bunch of nurses. To make matters worse, we'd forgotten the air freshener.

Our eyes were drawn first to the oak floor which was crawling with woodlice. It was Amy that spotted the dead mouse on the doormat. Its eyes had been eaten and it was teeming with lice. The mat beneath it rippled like black, shifting sand as the fleas scurried inside, their stiff host abandoned.

'What a welcome!' cursed Karen. Amy grabbed the mouse by its tail and flung it outside towards the black cat who, coincidentally, was sitting on the wall swinging its tail in jest.

We were in desperate need of cheering up. Any old excuse!

'Cocktail time!' said Liz, as she headed to the fridge.

'I'll check the hot tub,' Karen stated, marching outside.

I followed her, needing a breath of fresh air. A seagull was poised on the tub's lid, its beady eyes gazed skyward. Its pure, white feathers were plumped up which increased its size dramatically. Its neck stretched tautly and its yellow beak opened wide as it cried out in triumph laying claim to this territory. Karen was also territorial and charged towards it flapping her towel in battle. It put up a good fight but eventually flew off spraying white shit all over the lid as it soared away. 'Damn vermin!' she cursed. 'Flying rats! Let's get the lid off and check the water.'

Our shoulders slumped together, the water was filthy. The surface was covered with a thick, oily scum. Karen dropped the lid in temper and stormed back into the house.

'Look on the bright side,' I shouted. 'A man will have to come round and clean it.' Minutes later, I was eavesdropping on her phone call as she frustratedly blurted out her complaint to an answerphone. She slammed the phone down in exasperation which blocked out her profanities.

We joined the others at the table and gave them the bad news. Anyone might think a world war had been declared or alcohol banned. However, the piña coladas soon worked wonders and the hot tub was forgotten for the time being.

'We'll do wine tasting instead,' Karen suggested with renewed enthusiasm but Jill had good reason to change the subject.

'Gosh! Look at the roses!' she gasped, reaching for the vase in horror. The petals scattered as she checked the water level. The beautifully scented bouquet we'd left this morning was now a mass of dry, drooping flowers. She was well and truly flabbergasted, as we all were. 'They've got water. How on earth could they get in that state in just a few hours?'

We all agreed it was strange. Amy put extra tots of rum in the drinks to help us commiserate.

'This house is weird,' declared Emma taking a huge slurp of the cocktail. The room was silent until the straws gurgled as we all sucked up the dregs in our glasses.

It was a tradition that on a Saturday night we would all glam up. It was one of the best parts of the weekend, particularly cherished by Mo who came alive at the sight of a hairdryer. There had been a near miss one year in the early days when we could only afford cheap accommodation. Dodgy wiring had caused Mo's new hairdryer to burst into flames. I shuddered at the thought, albeit mostly at the thought of the good-looking electrician that had come round.

There'd been some laughs over the years, experimenting with make-up, hairstyles and outfits. There had been a few arguments as well. Although we considered ourselves good friends, and we all asked for honest opinions, sometimes honesty was not wholly appreciated. It soon became apparent that none of us liked being told that a bigger size would look better. Being accused of lying about missing labels, sizes and prices certainly did not go down well either. Two of the group actually didn't speak for several weeks after that argument.

It was quite a skill choosing a dress able to withstand Saturday evening antics as there was always a lot of dancing and if Amy had her way we would have to endure at least an hour of the game Twister. Price and comfort were, therefore, prioritised as well as glitz and glamour. None of us wanted to split or damage an expensive dress. This year it would be easier. There would most definitely be less stress and less competition.

Amy and I had been on a shopping trip and had come across a market stall filled with elaborately patterned dresses. It was closing down so all the dresses were the same price. We couldn't believe our luck! We'd come away laughing and gloating with excitement and dread at what the others would say. On the spur of the moment, we had purchased eight medium-sized maxi dresses so there could be no arguments. Surprisingly, the coffee morning meeting had gone smoothly when we'd all picked a colour. They were polyester, off-shoulder, elastic-waisted, generously sized, which fulfilled all of our requirements.

'Perfect choice,' they'd all agreed.

'Gross,' we'd heard Emma whisper.

'Accessories and shoes can make an outfit,' Mo had lectured, so we'd all gone to town in that respect.

Upstairs buzzed with laughter and excitement as we all got ready, each of us nursing a large glass of prosecco to assist the process and enhance our exuberance. I was ready first so I made my way downstairs.

'Anyone need a top-up?' I shouted.

The temperature seemed to drop, stair by stair, as did the light. It was like entering a different world. The silence was eerie. My skin tingled as the hairs stood on end. My heart surely skipped a beat as my bare feet touched the floor at the bottom of the stairs. The carpet felt wet, ice-cold, but it was the quietness and the chill that seemed to penetrate my bones and unnerve me the most.

I had a profound awareness that someone was watching me.

But as quickly as this feeling had emerged, it subsided, and instead, curiosity took over. I touched the carpet with my hand, it was dry but I was taken aback suddenly by the acrid smell. It was coming from this very spot.

Looking around, the daylight now faded, the hallway had become a drab, gloomy place. Thick cobwebs hung like smog from the cornices. This windy passageway was most certainly grim. The sights that drew me in were grotesque and unsightly. Freezing wind hurtled through the letterbox denting any optimism. A cockroach scurried across the carpet. I nearly jumped out of my skin when Karen tapped me on the shoulder.

'The wine needs preparing for the tasting competition,' she stated, rushing into the kitchen, totally oblivious to my quandary.

We all looked good. Mo was right, the little touches and accessories had truly enhanced the dresses. Our hair and make-up looked professionally done and completed the package, making us a 'bevvy of beauties' as we'd once been called by a drunk staggering from the pub.

There were some sassy shoes on show. Vanity to the extreme. I noticed that someone had shortened their hem to ensure their shoes would be seen and admired. Their dress was now much too short, I smirked. It wasn't Karen. She never wanted her shoes on show and she had good reason. They were bought for comfort and comfort alone. I could tell Emma was pleasantly surprised at the turnout as she was anxious to take a picture.

'Beautiful!' she cooed as she sorted the selfie stick. We made our way to the window seat, proseccos in hand, for our annual photo. This was one of our most favoured traditions and the window seat was the ideal setup. The lighting was perfect.

The view from the window had changed again. It was as if an artist had painted the same landscape using different colours to create a different scene, depending on mood and time of day. This picture depicted a storm brewing at sunset as the blood-red sky at the forefront held back a mass of black storm clouds that loomed in the background like a tidal wave. The sun, now low, was hidden behind the dark, domineering clouds. Its reddish hue dared to tint them on the edges as if that's all they would allow.

Sensing the incoming storm, flocks of gulls flew in circles on the thermals. Far on the horizon, the lightning flickered turning the sky gold for an instant but there was no thunder. The storm was miles away. A murmuration of starlings hovered like a shadow high above the house, dimming the light and adding to my anxiety as that particular wonder of nature was unusual for this time of year.

'Cheer up,' said Karen as she set the covered bottles of wine at the head of the table.

I snapped out of my gloomy mood feigning a smile for my sake and theirs. It was the hallway. It had really gotten under my skin.

We all sat around the table awaiting instruction. Pens and paper had been placed neatly by each of us, along with large wine glasses. For the sake of sensibility, there was a large jug of iced water in the centre of the table along with a spittle bowl and tissues.

Karen instructed us most formally. 'Anyone cheating or supping more than a mouthful will be penalised,' she chided whilst looking at Amy accusingly.

It turned out to be a great activity and was actually taken very seriously. I think secretly we all wanted to prove our etiquette and show that we could tell the difference between cheap plonk and top-notch quality. I observed Karen's devious side at play as she dropped hints and made approving noises or a displeasing face when she tasted the wine. I knew she would try to lead Amy astray. We were all having a great time, relaxed and tipsy. Incidentally, there wasn't much wine in the spittle bowl.

The results were in.

Karen's plan had worked. Amy had rated the pinot grigio as her favourite. That was normally the only white wine she refused to drink. Karen's gloating was short-lived as the expensive chardonnay she'd bought in France came second from the bottom. The laughing and joking continued as we topped up our glasses.

'These candles won't light!' moaned Liz before giving up, declaring that the wicks were damp.

We set the table with some nibbles whilst the chefs cooked our supper. The smell of fresh garlic and herbs wafted around the room whetting our appetites. Karen's mushroom stroganoff was always delicious. Whilst we knew the main ingredients, the exact amounts were a closely guarded secret so no one could ever make it like her. Several of us had been scolded in the past for suggesting dried thyme instead of fresh.

This year we noticed she was using lots of different mushrooms, as well as the usual copious amounts of butter. It would be presented with a swirl of cream then garnished with fresh herbs. Sour cream instead of double made it healthier, she lectured us. It was always served on a bed of wild rice. She never used plain. I remembered with a smile the fiasco that had occurred the year Jill had accidentally ordered microwavable rice in a bag.

Whilst we waited for dinner, Emma put the music on and began dishing out musical instruments which her husband Gary had bought us. She had a good catch there. We were tired of karaoke, especially as none of us could sing, and he must have taken that on board.

Maybe the men feared the trips might stop if we got bored and their respite might come to an end.

We all rushed forward like a sale had been announced. We all fancied the tambourine, no one wanted the triangle. 'Calm down!' she chastised. It was just as well they weren't proper instruments. Amy had got the mouth organ much to everyone's annoyance.

'I'll hide that the first chance I get,' Karen whispered, screwing up her face in pain.

'Time for some pre-dinner dancing,' Liz slurred, swinging her hips and downing her wine.

I pranced around the room, completely out of rhythm, shaking the maracas above my head. I was very woozy. Mo was asleep sitting up, still holding the triangle. We'd had a lot of alcohol and relatively little food. I knew that was foolish. I'm sure we all did. I cursed Karen's wine tasting. Why didn't we wait 'til after supper?

Something caught my eye as I danced around the kitchen. The rice in the jar seemed to be moving with the music like shifting sand. On closer inspection, I was horrified.

'Turn the music off,' I shouted. I peered into the jar, the basmati rice was crawling with maggots. Jill was beside me now with her reading glasses on.

'Revolting!' she stuttered, recoiling in horror. They all gathered around in total disbelief. Amy grabbed the jar and rushed out into the garden throwing the grisly contents into the flower border. 'Feed the birds!' she sang at the top of her voice. Her impersonation of Julie Andrews was remarkably good considering she was as pissed as the rest of us.

'Thank goodness we're having wild rice,' said Karen shaking her head. Though she was swaying, she sounded sober and she spoke sternly and coherently. 'I will be reporting this place to Health and Safety first thing Monday morning. You mark my words!'

Supper was soon served. We definitely needed food to soak up the alcohol. We were all starving, as usual. No one had lost their appetite, despite the maggots. Unfortunately, large glasses of red wine replaced the white which was now all gone. We had large glasses of water as a token gesture. The stroganoff didn't disappoint. It was delicious and we all had seconds.

'Even better this year,' said Mo prodding her last mushroom with a fork. 'How many different types or is that a secret as well?'

If Karen heard her, she didn't answer. She was engrossed on her phone asking for Google's advice. 'I expect that rice has been here for months, a blowfly must've laid eggs and they've hatched out in the heat,' she suddenly announced.

'Yes, I agree,' said Amy, tugging my arm and hinting that I follow her outside. Although she was au fait with decaying bodies, she had nothing further to add. She'd allow Karen to be a maggot expert for the time being. The others sat bloated and bleary-eyed on the sofa, dozing.

They were oblivious to our disappearance.

# CHAPTER 9

We tentatively made our way to the bench in the back garden. It was dark and humid, the day's heat trapped by the huge cumulus clouds above. No stars for comfort tonight.

The bats flew back and forth; their skilful aerobatics provided a nighttime extravaganza around the lamp as they captured the moths. The cat was sitting on a rock shelf, a black imprint on the grey slate. Its green eyes were just visible and its stare was disconcerting.

'No red eyes tonight,' said Amy looking up at the bird hide. 'I'm getting freaked out about this house. There's something not right,' she continued. 'Do you think we should tell the others about what the barmaid told us? It's a coincidence that she lives next door, don't you think? She failed to mention that yesterday.'

'I agree. It's all a bit strange, creepy if I'm honest. I think we should tell them in the morning when we're all sober.' Satisfied with the compromise, we sat enjoying the cool night air. The only downside was that it was thick with mosquitoes. Hopefully, we wouldn't get bitten to death. I wondered if they would get drunk on our blood if we did.

The wind was gaining momentum and the sound of the waves crashing on the rocks was getting louder and more powerful. There'll be a storm tonight, for sure. Amy was talking to herself, rambling on and on. I noticed she was having difficulty stringing her words together and I automatically blamed the alcohol.

I looked around. I was feeling giddy myself, claustrophobic, the cliff appeared to close in around us like a massive gorge towering skyward. I glanced downwards, the ground seemed to be rocking like a ship on a stormy sea. The roar of the ocean heightened the effect. Bats whirled around our heads, spinning faster and faster, whipping up the wind like a tornado. A wave of nausea hit me, I put my head between my legs to fight off an impending faint. I was clammy, palpitations pounded inside my chest and my stomach lurched.

Amy looked awful. The lamplight shone directly on her face, enhancing her paleness. Her appearance was ghostly. Her eyes looked hollow and glazed and there were dark rings beneath them. She too was clammy, beads of perspiration glistened on her forehead. We had drunk far too much again, I cursed to myself.

'Come on, we need some water.'

I pulled her up and we staggered towards the house. The ground beneath us seemed to shift as we walked, hindering us. I just caught sight of the red eyes in the window next door. They were bigger this time, with a steely gaze that didn't leave us. The stare was arrogant and threatening, no attempt was made to hide this time, whoever it was wanted to be seen. But it was the smiling mouth that scared me the most.

The cold hallway was welcome and the usual odour was masked by the sweet scent of musk. I was most grateful for someone's thoughtful intervention. I steered Amy into the lounge in a somewhat haphazard fashion and we flopped down on the sofa with the others. I was feeling very drunk, in fact, I was feeling as high as a kite. Looking at the glazed eyes and slumped postures of the others, I'm pretty sure we all felt the same.

That spaced-out feeling took me back to what had happened on our first trip together in the tent ten years beforehand. Looking back now it seemed like we were trying to relive our youths, or some of us were. After all, most of us had got married and had children at an early age.

It was a wonder that we kept or salvaged our careers as it was much harder for women even a decade ago.

'You ok?' asked Amy, waving her hands in front of my face.

'No, I feel really drunk.'

'Me too,' she slurred as she went to get us some more water.

I peered around the swaying room, it looked like they'd all passed out and been frozen in time. Only Jill was moving, slowly patting the tambourine in a trance-like state, her eyes were fixed, staring ahead like a zombie. Amy came wobbling back in, precariously balancing a tray with big glasses of water on.

'Wakey wakey!' she shouted, grabbing the tambourine and violently shaking it above her head.

'I'm pissed!' laughed Liz, staggering to her feet before chanting to the music. Emma had put on Dancing Queen which she knew would get us all up. We all had our signature moves and they would definitely be on display tonight judging by the way Amy was pointing to the ceiling almost down on one knee. The stretchy dresses were an excellent choice. The instruments had been revived, apart from the mouth organ which had gone missing. Margaritas soon appeared, as if by magic, and we all danced around the room.

The music was getting louder and louder, the dance moves were exaggerated beyond imagination, testing limbs and the dresses to the very limit. No splits yet! I suddenly found myself in the middle of the room, cushions were shoved up my dress around my backside. I realised I was doing impressions of our old boss. It was as if someone had taken over my body. The laughter was hysterical, which egged me on. Fleetwood Mac's 'Tusk' and alcohol intoxication coaxed them all to join in, inhibitions were well and truly abandoned.

As I spun around in hysterics, I saw it. I wasn't the only one. The scream rang out in time with the music. I stopped dead in my tracks.

Emma had jumped onto the sofa and was clutching a cushion in front of her face. The beat continued, as did the dancing. I was frozen centre stage waiting for it to move, convincing myself that I was seeing things as everything was blurry. Then it moved. The scream rang out again and this time it was heard. They all saw it together which made things worse. The music had stopped and, like musical chairs, they all dived onto the settee. Amy and I stood there paralysed, staring in disbelief.

'Oh my God! Is it real?' cried Liz.

The huge spider was motionless halfway up the wall by the mantlepiece. Its legs were so long they made shadows on the white wall and its eyes glistened like black pearls. Its grey body was at least two inches long.

'It's massive!' screamed Emma in terror.

Karen edged off the sofa and tiptoed over to us with her phone. She managed to take a photo but the spider was startled by the flash and made a hasty retreat under the mantlepiece and up the chimney. We all screamed again as we heaped together on the sofa.

'It's the one I saw in the bathroom,' spluttered Emma.

'They don't like bright lights,' said Amy reaching for the light switch. As the lounge illuminated, our courage momentarily returned and we rushed out slamming the lounge door tightly shut. We would never go in there again.

We gathered around the table in the dining room and consulted Google. We agreed unanimously that it was probably a giant huntsman spider. Though not poisonous, they can give a painful bite and they are known to frequent houses in warm, tropical climates. Definitely not southwest England, even in the summer!

'The good news is that it eats cockroaches and lives in crevices, so hopefully, it'll stay up the chimney,' said Karen looking at her phone. 'Oh, and it doesn't make a web so there's no excuse for all the cobwebs!'

Emma had put some chill-out music on and Jill had poured us large glasses of water to clear our heads. We were all surprisingly calm, even Emma, considering what we'd just witnessed but I knew the alcohol had numbed our senses.

After a spate of frenzied texting and then a short period of quiet contemplation, we all became very animated. It was quite frustrating as we were all trying to talk at the same time. In fact, we were too upbeat considering what we'd just witnessed. Emma kept reiterating that the lounge door must be kept shut. She'd wedged a towel along the bottom of the door to ensure the spider couldn't get out. I was up for a challenge and was secretly considering returning to the lounge to investigate and maybe even capture it. Adrenaline had kicked in and it was most definitely fight not flight. Fleetwood Mac was back on and so was the dancing, everyone seemed to have a new lease of life. I was feeling great until nausea crept in and spoilt things. The way the room kept spinning was disorientating. I suddenly felt very sick so I hurried to the bathroom.

Dizziness overwhelmed me and I steadied myself at the sink. I splashed cold water on my face willing myself to feel better. In fact, I felt quite the contrary. As I dried my eyes, I was confronted with my reflection in the mirror. I stifled my scream with the towel. The reflection staring back was hideous, a grotesque form of me with exaggerated features. A nose protruded from the mirror to touch my nose, its coldness was vicious and I flinched. The eyes stretched horizontally, flattening the forehead into an ugly deformity. The towel I clutched resembled a snake coiled tightly around my neck and mouth, suffocating me, squeezing my life away. I couldn't breathe.

'You ok?' said Rachel bursting into the bathroom and shattering the illusion.

'I'm fine,' I stammered as my normal reflection pulled me back to reality. However, my anxiety returned when I entered the macabre hallway. The rancid smell had returned. The music stopped suddenly, as did I so I could listen intently to the sound of the wind chimes which whistled hauntingly outside.

They were all sat around the table, each nursing a large glass of water. A somewhat incoherent debate had begun about the state of the house, the strange occurrences and, of course, the spider. Arguments were emerging about the cocktails being made too strong and Amy was complaining that the wine was thirteen percent when she usually only drank eleven percent proof. I grabbed some water and joined the discussion. We all couldn't fathom why we were feeling so spaced out, which was ridiculous really considering the number of drinks we'd consumed.

'It's pure and simple - alcohol intoxication,' lectured Karen counting up the empty bottles. 'When will we ever learn?' she chastised shaking her head and glaring at Liz this time as she had made the cocktails. We all looked rough, Mo in particular. She eased herself up and was very unsteady on her feet.

'You ok?' asked Rachel, grabbing her arm.

'I'm fine, just a bit nauseous. Just going to the loo.' Jill followed her out to check she got there.

'I'll make some coffees and maybe we can play Scrabble,' Karen suggested.

'My vision's too blurred,' whined Emma and we all agreed, shaking our heads like nodding dogs on a car shelf.

'What about Twister?' piped up Amy. Nobody answered.

We all jumped as the rain lashed down on the window panes. It was hailstones, for sure, as the glass was hammered so ferociously we feared it would shatter. A flash of lightning startled us soon after. The crackle of thunder was ear-splitting, shaking the foundations and moving the table. The lights all dimmed and the ice cubes rattled in the jug of water. We were plunged into darkness for a few short seconds.

The microwave beeped as the power surged back and the lights came on. I noticed the hallway was still in darkness and discovered the bulb was blown. The landing light was flickering above. The light it produced was like moonlight and it illuminated the shapes on the wallpaper, turning them into mystical creatures with eyes that followed me. The lightning flashed again, creating strange shadows all along the hallway. I was getting the heebie-jeebies. Well, I was shitting it to be more exact.

'Hurry up, Mo!' I shouted, too frightened to venture any further.

Someone had the foresight to make coffee which was just what we needed. We were all huddled around the table. The temperature had dropped dramatically and the humidity had gone but there was tension in the air. We all looked around together as Mo came through the door. She just stood there, one hand gripping the door frame. She was deathly pale and her eyes were vacant.

'Whatever is the matter?' asked Amy, getting up in alarm. 'You look like you've seen a ghost!'

In an instant, Mo had fallen. Her legs gave way, her body crumpled and she smashed her head on the corner of the glass coffee table before hitting the ground.

'Oh, shit!' cried Rachel.

# CHAPTER 10

It was just like an emergency drill.

We had all practised those hundreds of times before and had experienced the real thing. She'd landed on her side and there was blood gushing from a head wound. She appeared to be unconscious.

Rachel knelt down to see if she responded. 'Mo,' she called, gently shaking her. I checked her airway which was clear. There was silence as I looked for breathing, feeling for breath whilst observing her chest. A sigh of relief sounded as we all saw positive signs.

Karen felt her carotid for a pulse. There was silence again as she counted the beats. Her pulse was slow and thready, she informed us in a shaky voice. This kind of situation was always stressful even more so if it was someone you knew, let alone a best friend or work colleague.

'Vasovagal,' I murmured calmly, which meant she had probably fainted. My voice sounded calm, quite the contrary to how I felt inside. Rachel attempted to rouse her but to no avail. It was all very stressful, even for trained professionals.

'Call 999 please, Jill,' ordered Karen. 'I'm not taking any chances.'

I felt panicked. Our predicament was self-inflicted, I was sure. The amount of alcohol we'd consumed was more than foolhardy, it was downright dangerous!

Jill rushed over to the window to make the call.

Liz had retrieved a first aid box from the car and was gloved up. She had a wad of gauze to suppress the bleeding and managed to gently assess the wound without moving her.

'She's definitely going to need stitches,' she said. Liz was an expert suturer, though heads were not her usual area of expertise. I smiled as I saw Emma with pen and paper writing down the times and sequence of events. Conditioned behaviour at its very best.

Jill came off the phone after answering a barrage of questions. We had been allocated a category 1 ambulance or a 'blue light' due to bleeding and unconsciousness.

'Rightly so!' piped up Karen, still monitoring Mo's pulse.

'Let's see what their response time is like out in the sticks!' I nodded to Emma who was poised, pen in hand. Amy was on the lookout for the blue lights.

'Mo,' called Rachel again, 'can you hear us?'

I knelt down and felt her skin. She was cold, clammy and pale but no cyanosis. Remembering neuro obs, I pinched her earlobe as part of the process of assessing her level of consciousness and awareness. She started to stir and moan and nearly frightened us half to death by opening her eyes very suddenly. I noticed straight away that her pupils were very dilated even though the light in the room was bright.

'They're here,' shouted Amy from the hallway.

'Bloody well done,' Emma praised. 'Eight minutes! Bang on target!'

The blue lights flashed through the curtains like a macabre disco light. Jill had the foresight to have tidied up, thank goodness. All the empties had been shoved in a cupboard. A large beach towel covered the recycling crate.

'Evening ladies! What has happened here then?' the paramedic asked as he marched in with his kit and his partner in tow.

Karen relayed the events in minute detail, leaving out the amount of alcohol we'd consumed. I picked out the sentence, 'We've all had a few glasses of wine with our meal.'

That was swiftly followed by, 'We think she fainted and fell but we aren't sure if the loss of consciousness was due to the head injury.'

'Been out have you?!' he chuckled, looking at our dresses.

'No,' Karen answered firmly as her face flushed from the neck upwards.

'Well, she's fully conscious now,' he said as he questioned Mo.

'She wasn't when we made the call,' stated Amy stepping forward, hand on hip. Her nose was red and shiny, matching her ruddy cheeks, a stark contrast to her paleness earlier.

The paramedic kept Mo immobilised and carried out his assessment. I noticed his partner looking around the room and smirking in a friendly way. Emma had an odd look on her face, I realised she was sat on an empty gin bottle. She began to giggle uncontrollably. Highly inappropriate. I responded by giving her a dirty look.

'Girly weekend?' he inquired, smiling.

'Yes,' I replied and then I broke the rule. 'We work in the NHS actually and we treat ourselves to a break once a year.' We had all agreed it was best to keep our professions to ourselves on weekends away. And this sort of situation was precisely why.

'Nurses I bet?!' piped up Dave, his partner.

'Yes and midwives!' I added. There were smiles all around and the atmosphere changed immediately. We were all one big family.

They fetched the stretcher as Dave had concluded after a thorough examination that she was safe to move. She would need an X-ray and monitoring due to the head wound which would need suturing at the very least. He was also concerned, like us, about the visual disturbances that she was reporting. She was bound to have a concussion and one hell of a hangover. He had also commented on her dilated pupils.

It was pouring with rain and the wind howled both inside and out. It was absurd weather for May. They were shocked when they opened the door, as instead of the gale lashing rain into the house the opposite happened. An icy blast almost swept the stretcher away as a strong gust of wind raced out the doorway.

'Christ!' he cursed. 'Have you got the back door open?'

'It's a windy passageway,' shouted Karen.

'You can say that again,' he replied.

We had decided between us that Karen and I would go with Mo to the hospital. We transferred to the ambulance as quickly as possible as it was pouring down. I noticed the gap in the curtains next door and sensed that we were being watched, although the house was in darkness.

I almost lost my footing as I climbed into the back of the ambulance. My vision was blurred again and I felt nauseous. I sighed with relief at the familiar territory. I buckled up, relieved to be in a forward-facing seat. It wouldn't take much to make me vomit. Karen was in the front with Steve the driver.

Mo was strapped in and rigged up for monitoring. She was propped up with pillows but her eyes were tightly closed. Her face was ashen. She looked awful. I touched her arm and wasn't surprised that her skin remained cold and clammy, in fact, mine wasn't much better.

I had done a lot of ambulance transfers over the years but never once imagined this scenario. I was embarrassed. We all were. Alcohol had played its part and, worse still, Dave kept on about her dilated pupils and fast heart rate. Drugs. I knew what he was hinting at but that was something we would never do...at least not intentionally!

I looked at all the equipment to take my mind off things. I scanned the monitor noticing that everything was all within normal limits apart from her fast heart rate, sinus tachycardia. Oxygen saturation was improving thanks to the oxygen they'd put her on due to her poor colour. She still felt cold so I pulled the blanket up around her. Blood pressure was normal, probably a bit on the low side for Mo. I'd check her pupils when she woke up.

My thoughts were broken by Dave reaching for a vomit bowl. He passed it through to the front as apparently Karen was feeling nauseous. Now that was highly unusual. She, like myself, was used to bumpy transfers and apart from her high pain threshold she also possessed what she referred to as an 'iron stomach'. She often boasted that she'd never ever vomited, and nausea, like tiredness, was a mere state of mind. It wasn't just waffle. In her thirty years in the NHS, she had never had a day off sick. Deserved a bloody medal, we all often told her.

I felt dizzy and was experiencing some mild palpitations. I closed my eyes trying to quell the feeling. When I opened my eyes, my heart raced even faster. Dave was leaning back in his seat facing me but his face had disappeared. He was featureless. A black hole opened where his mouth belonged.

'Are you ok?' I heard him say as we pulled into A & E.

My memories of the next few hours were patchy. I had fallen asleep on two chairs and the next thing I knew Karen was coaxing me to drink a bottle of water and was eager to fill me in. I realised that two hours had gone by. I was glad that I'd actually been asleep as I caught sight of my reflection in the window, the dresses looked absolutely ridiculous. She informed me that she'd rung a taxi to take us home, not bad going considering it was a Saturday night.

Unsurprisingly, the care had been exceptional from start to finish. We'd been lucky as Mo had been triaged and seen before the pubs and clubs kicked out, not that there were many of those in this neck of the woods. They were keeping her in overnight for observation. Bloods had been taken and the X-ray had shown no fracture, thank goodness. The suturing had been painful but her alcohol level definitely helped and she'd actually got a fit of the giggles much to the displeasure of the junior doctor.

We went to say our goodbyes and assured her we would be back in the morning, but as we were about to leave she grabbed my arm and looked me directly in the eyes. She was edgy and her tone of voice was deadly serious.

'There was someone at the top of the stairs.' I felt my haunches raise and the hairs on the back of my neck followed suit.

'We need to get back as soon as possible,' I said to Karen, dragging her out of the door.

# CHAPTER 11

We sat together in the back of the taxi. I pondered for all of five minutes then decided to come clean, well, partially. I relayed the tragic story that the barmaid had told Amy and me at the pub. I was conscious that the taxi driver might be listening so I spoke as quickly and as quietly as I could. I failed to mention what Mo had said about seeing a man at the top of the stairs. I thought she was seeing things, like myself, so I put it to the back of my mind. After all, I had been hallucinating and I hadn't had a blow to the head. I needed to take things one step at a time where Karen was concerned.

Luckily the radio was playing as this harrowing information was for her ears only. It was difficult as she kept asking me to repeat the gory details because she couldn't believe what she was hearing. She took a while to take it all in. Her response was both guarded and contrite and not wholly what I wanted to hear.

Karen reluctantly agreed that the house was creepy and there were some strange anomalies but she refused to entertain the fact that it was anything other than vivid imagination and paranoia induced by the disgraceful amount of alcohol we'd all consumed. The hallway, however, was definitely up for debate. She remained stoic but gave an inch, admitting that she, like myself, had been freaked out by the weird shapes and shadows along the hallway and up the stairs. There was no denying that there was a giant huntsman spider in the lounge as we had all seen it and we had a photo to prove the fact.

Mixing alcohol had been a fatal mistake, no wonder there had been shenanigans and an accident. Intoxicated minds were easy pickings, delusion and paranoia were to be expected as far as Karen was concerned. Her analysis was given with staunch conviction and it explained Mo's subsequent fall. 'End of matter,' she added with finality.

I was unconvinced and stared out of the window in silent acquiescence. She sensed my mood and nudged me, more leeway I hoped.

'However, the putrid smell and ice-cold air is inexplicable,' she whispered. 'I suggest we all discuss it tomorrow as a group.'

By the time we reached the house, fatigue had surrendered me to her way of thinking. After all, I had experienced a horrendous hallucination in the ambulance which had nothing to do with the house.

She was suddenly dozing off, her posture was slumped and awkward and her skin looked pasty and clammy. I had never seen Karen looking ill before in all the years I'd known her. It was a phenomenon in itself and most disconcerting.

'I feel like crap,' she mumbled. 'My head's throbbing and everything looks so bloody bright!' Bad language as well, which was totally out of character.

They were all still up when we got back, huddled together around the table waiting for news about Mo. The stress of the evening's events had taken their toll and aged their faces, they looked drained and I'm sure I did. It was almost one o'clock in the morning and we were all shattered so Karen and I quickly filled them in on Mo's hospital encounter.

We agreed unanimously that a small Baileys before bed was acceptable considering the diabolical evening we'd endured.

'I'll water it down with extra ice,' said Rachel, presumably trying to be sensible.

We were all feeling odd, not just drunk. The snippets of symptoms, like nausea and palpitations, were common side effects of alcohol abuse but it was the hallucinations and muscle cramps that played on my mind. I knew I was in for a restless night.

'Let's call it a day and hope for a better one tomorrow,' said Liz, clearing away the glasses.

I think it must have been the first time we walked through that sinister hallway without a grumble. We were all too tired and too spaced out to notice if there was anything untoward.

I lingered on the landing after they had all finished in the bathroom. The wind whistled outside and the rain poured down relentlessly, battering the window panes. Thick, black clouds raced across the moon, darkening and lightening the staircase like a strobe light. I could feel the cold air creeping up the stairs as if to seek me out. It must be blowing in through the letterbox, I rationalised to reassure myself. I could see the letterbox, however, and there was no rattling. It looked tightly shut.

For a minute the moon owned the night sky as the clouds blew by and a soft silver hue shimmered in...

But it revealed a vision that I didn't want to see.

For a few terrifying seconds, it appeared at the bottom of the stairs.

A huge viscous puddle. This time it wasn't dark mulberry like wine. It was the unmistakable bright red of arterial blood. It vanished in an instant and the jolt from my heartbeat bolstered me into my room.

Amy was fast asleep, hardly visible under the duvet. Her snoring was soothing. My panic subsided and I flopped into bed and prayed that sleep would whisk me away from this madness but it wasn't that simple.

At some point, sleep found me. The rain was now a gentle patter on the window and thunder rumbled in the distance. I could hear the sea, stormy and angry, in harmony with the sound of a guitar. It seemed to strum in time with the waves. The chords hollered out in tempest, stirring me to heed their warning. I tossed and turned like a raft on the sea as deep sleep eluded me and the night dragged on.

Then I was suddenly in the dining room, a noise must have led me there. What a mess I encountered, rubbish strewn everywhere. Something had been in the bin and the culprit was on the table - that seagull. It was helping itself to the last of the honey-roasted peanuts.

'You bastard!' I sneered. 'My favourites!'

It didn't stand a chance, the speed with which I moved. Before I knew it, my hands were round its neck. I squeezed tightly, preventing the beak from gashing me. I dragged it like a piping bag spewing icing along the hallway. Reaching the garden, I grabbed its feet with one hand as it struggled. I swirled it around my head like a lasso with such force that when I let go it hit the rocks above. Down it fell, feathers raining like snow. There was a loud thud as it hit the ground.

I woke with such a start that my body jerked like it was me falling. Glancing at the clock on the bedside table I realised I had only been in bed no more than an hour or two. I willed sleep to return. My head was throbbing and my muscles ached with fatigue.

When I woke again, I was lying on my side facing the wall. The air was still and silent and I wondered with apprehension what had woken me.

I was sweating profusely. I closed my eyes tightly to listen, willing a sound to break the claustrophobic tension.

The silence became more sinister. Absence of creaks from the old house and the fact that the wind and rain had disappeared only added to my anxiety. Amy had no breath sounds and nor did I as I held mine in terror. There was just nothingness. A tremendous sense of impending doom fell upon the room and terrified me. My rigid state was painful, every sinew and muscle ached with tension until I plucked up the courage to open my eyes.

The wall in front of me shifted forward in a truly dramatic fashion. It was now almost touching my nose. My heart pounded in my ribcage. The wall retreated as I began to hyperventilate. A flash of lightning illuminated the room and I saw the shadow of what was behind me.

'Now you will die,' came from the depths of my mind. A thunderbolt crackled like a starting gun and the adrenaline made me turn to face the demon.

Amy was sitting on the edge of the bed staring directly at me, her hair stood on end.

A nervous snigger emerged spontaneously at the memory of the Rod Stewart concert we attended but terror returned to consume me as her form revealed itself. I could only see the whites of her eyes but it was the smile that was forming and the furrowed brow that broke me. She looked like a lunatic, eyelids flickering as she started to laugh.

The power of my scream was awesome and they all came running this time. It was as if I had pulled the emergency bell.

'Lie her on her left side,' stammered Karen. 'She's having some sort of fit.'

Amy screamed when Karen touched her, scaring them all senseless.

'It's just a bloody nightmare,' screeched Liz stomping off.

Rachel muttered under her breath and followed suit.

Amy staggered up rubbing her eyes, trying in vain to retrieve her contact lenses.

'Drama over!' tutted Karen retreating with the others.

Amy shut up eventually. The gibbering was replaced by deep, throaty snoring. I wrapped the pillow around my ears. When the snoring eventually subsided, it was tranquil. I languished in the blissful silence knowing that the dawn chorus approached.

The old house seemed to come alive. Its timbers creaked and stretched like stiff, arthritic limbs. I stretched, trying to banish the dull ache that persisted throughout my whole body, and then I heard that queer noise again. The scraping sound was out of place. Quietness soon resumed as did the soft rhythmic patter of tiptoes above, which for some obscure reason soothed me. It must be birds, or mice, or maybe a squirrel.

We'd had a squirrel nesting in the loft when I was a kid, as painfully curious as I was now.

# CHAPTER 12

We all overslept and had raging hangovers, there were no denials this time. I made it downstairs eventually and was happy to hear from Karen that Mo was being discharged later in the morning. We all kept straight faces as her tone was super serious, even though she was clutching a J-cloth to her temple and wearing her old glasses with ultra-thick lenses.

'Lost your contacts?' sniggered Amy.

'That's rich coming from you,' Karen retorted, 'waking us all up in the early hours!'

'To be fair, it was my scream,' I admitted.

There was a large jug of squash in the centre of the table and I could smell fresh coffee and toast. Rachel had that on the go as she was the bringer of bad news.

'There will be no cooked breakfast this morning,' she announced curtly as if it was a punishment. And that it was! I knew from past experience that a fry-up was a good cure for a hangover and that was backed up by countless studies that had done the research. Rachel sighed and made a point of tightening the bandage on her knee. All was forgiven.

My whole body ached and my head felt like it was in a vice.

'I feel like a sack of shit!' grizzled Liz, nearly in tears.

The sun streamed in through the window accentuating our headaches and sensitising our eyes. Thinking better of her outburst, Liz had put her sunglasses on and was now doing the rounds dabbing peppermint oil on our foreheads to restore the equilibrium. The paracetamol packet had been reinstated and lay half-empty on the table. Headache aside, I had the sudden urge to laugh at the sight of us. Whatever did we expect, we'd played fast and loose once too often and age was against us now.

'Shall I take a photo to remind us of our folly?' I said to Emma who had collapsed on the window seat. She had cucumber slices covering her eyes and her hair was a wild, untamed ball of frizz. No one answered my question but Karen's filthy look said it all.

Amy attempted her morning stretches. She looked like she had just got off a mortuary slab. She moaned in pain with each move and rubbed her back as if she was in agony. 'What a sorry state!' she mumbled as we creaked around the room like a bunch of wooden dolls. It was the first time we had ever joined in with her morning exercise regime. We were desperate to get rid of the muscle pains and headaches so I think we were willing to try virtually anything. It was a shame as normally she would have been delighted with our efforts but today she couldn't care less.

Jill had her feet in a bowl of cold water to ease the swelling. Then someone said something really brave.

'Do you think there was something wrong with the food?' questioned Amy, eyeing Karen as she stretched.

Emma let out an almighty sigh and rolled over to face the window. She wrapped the cushion around her ears.

'Don't be so ridiculous!' scorned Karen in a temper, colour now flushing her pale face. 'What the fuck could go wrong with mushrooms?'

I wondered if she had been possessed by a foul-mouthed demon after such a churlish outburst.

Emma pulled herself up, her hair initially dazzled us as the sunlight streamed through before blocking out the sun entirely.

'There was a lot of static in the air last night,' I laughed as she gathered it into a ponytail.

'Calm yourselves,' soothed Rachel gently waving her hands downwards. 'There's no need for bickering, we are all to blame. We should know better by now.'

We all shut our eyes and dozed, quietly willing our bodies to rehydrate and recuperate. The only sound was the rhythmic ticking of the old clock. Emma must have gone out into the garden, presumably for some fresh air. Being quite a bit younger than us meant she would probably have a quicker recovery time and more so the fact that she didn't usually drink as much.

Minutes later her cry of alarm led us all there…

On the lid of the hot tub was a dead seagull.

'Aah!' she cried, 'He must've fallen off the cliff.'

'Really?' scoffed Karen. 'Birds can fly...or haven't you noticed? I think it's the one that has been hanging around,' she added. Her thick lenses reflected the sunlight like mini magnifying glasses, good job it was damp here as she was at risk of starting a fire.

'What do you think Amy?' We all said in unison as we knew she had witnessed many post-mortems and she had actually performed one on one of her chickens back home. We'd heard all about that, in great detail, several times.

We all stepped aside as she moved forward, eagerly putting on her glasses and rolling up her sleeves.

We waited in silence.

She took a deep breath, looked at it, paused and said, 'Yes, it's definitely dead.' She then began her examination.

'Eyes present and bright. I don't think it has been dead long, less than two hours I'd estimate. No head trauma.' Thank God, I thought.

'Gullet appears normal and the neck's not broken.'

She gently eased out each wing whilst mumbling, 'No breaks there, but the gut feels a bit distended.'

'So does mine,' groaned Liz.

'Errmmm...' Amy sighed slowly, scratching her head. 'Dirty tail feathers.'

We waited for the verdict in silence.

'I think he has been poisoned.' A sharp intake of breath came from us all.

'Poisoned?' gasped Emma. 'What a terrible way to die.' I could think of worse, remembering what had happened to my pet chicken. The less said about that the better.

'I disagree,' dared Jill forcing a straight face. 'I think it's the fall that killed him and he must've been frightened.'

'And how do you know that?' snarled Amy.

'Because he shit himself on the way down.' We all burst out laughing but soon fell silent as we were all animal lovers and hated the thought that he had suffered.

'Let's bury him in the garden,' suggested Emma.

'No! Definitely not! Get some cling film. We'll wrap him up to seal everything in, just in case it's bird flu. He'll stay fresh as well,' I joked.

'He was a good weight,' Karen said as she dropped the gull into the bin. I knew it was the seagull we had seen each day as I recognised the damaged webbing on its feet. Amy had missed that.

'Who would do such a thing?' asked Rachel with anger and suspicion as she glanced next door.

'I think we should go home,' Karen announced, sounding defeated.

That was when we all realised things were getting out of hand.

'Meeting,' said Rachel loudly as she marched back in. We reconvened around the table and topped up our coffees. Karen and I made eye contact and I nudged Amy. We conveyed the story that we had been told on Friday night. I decided that I ought to tell them about what Mo had said about seeing someone at the top of the stairs before she collapsed. It was all getting a bit dark for a supposed stress-free weekend break. This was certainly not what we would have envisaged. I explained that we hadn't told them about the death so at least some of us were spared the fact that a tragedy had occurred in this very house. They were all horrified, as expected. As the penny dropped, so did the language.

'Fuck!' said Rachel. 'What the hell's going on?'

'We need to do some digging and investigating,' I added, pacing around the table.

'Fuck!' cursed Liz. 'Do you think the hallway could be haunted?'

'Christ! That's two fucks and it's not even 11 o'clock. I ain't done that since I was seventeen!' Emma chipped in.

'Those were the days!' said Jill, pulling her tongue in.

Karen was getting very excited and I must admit some of this was giving me quite a thrill. The word 'haunted' must have had a positive effect on her as we all knew she was a fan of horror films. She used the adrenaline to her advantage. She was placing pens and paper by each of us with renewed enthusiasm so that we could brainstorm ideas and take notes. Her imagination, like mine, I'm sure, was in overdrive and it was catching. There was almost a buzz in the air. If anyone could fathom these mysterious happenings it would be us!

We wouldn't be going home after all.

After a good half hour of brainstorming, followed by a heated discussion, we decided that the main question that needed answering was whether or not the strange occurrences were connected to the supposed death of a man in the house, the weird neighbours, or both.

'Maybe the barmaid made the whole thing up?' said Emma.

'I don't believe in coincidences,' replied Karen with disdain. 'But I want to believe in ghosts.'

We all knew that she was deadly serious. A weekend vacation in a haunted house was on her bucket list, she had told us that on several occasions.

We had all written DEAD MAN at the top of our sheets of paper.

'Let's list anything strange we've noticed or experienced,' suggested Jill. 'No exaggeration or supposition, just facts.'

'This is just like consequences,' giggled Karen, relishing every moment and word. She was a massive fan of any sort of game and was fiercely competitive. So was Amy, but more so on the physical side so hopefully we could all work together without any arguing.

The house was almost silent as we concentrated on the task at hand. The only sound was our pens on the paper as we frantically scribbled down our thoughts. Hangovers were well and truly forgotten and so was Mo for the time being.

We all listed quite a few anomalies. In fact, the words and feelings we'd written down were all remarkably similar. Obviously, we had all been keeping things to ourselves which was most unusual.

Part of the reason we were all such good friends was the fact that we were all good listeners as well as talkers. If any of us had a concern, it was easy to start a discussion as we all trusted each other completely. With eight heads together, most problems would easily be solved or at least halved. Our friendship was something to cherish and I'm certain that's what we all did.

'Hugo Boss?!' scoffed Amy looking at Liz's paper. 'What's that all about?'

'I bet you cheated at exams,' sneered Karen in disgust.

'Aftershave,' Liz answered. 'I've smelt it several times. It's my favourite, Adam wears it all the time.' She went all dreamy at the thought.

We were lucky to have happy marriages, well, most of the time. I cringed at one particular memory. There had definitely been some ups and downs for all of us along the way but the divorce courts had been avoided thus far.

A further discussion, or rather debate, resulted in us crossing out most things. The majority of us decided that most of the peculiarities could be reasonably explained or be put down to confusion or paranoia due to the influence of alcohol.

'PISSED' remained underlined at the top of the page to ensure we all bore that in mind. I wasn't one of the majority but I went with the flow for the time being. 'HALLUCINATIONS' had been crossed out as Karen insisted that much of it was imagination which was a totally different thing altogether. This was turning out to be a briefing!

However, there were still quite a few things worthy of deliberation. We had all written SPIDER in block capitals. Rachel was the only one who had noticed the loft hatch slightly open in the middle of the night but she couldn't remember which night or if it was actually during the night. Karen put a line through it, blaming the wind.

An hour later we were left with five things that intrigued us: MAN, SPIDER, SMELL, RED EYES and AFTERSHAVE.

'My goodness! Look at the time,' interrupted Liz. 'We need to get Mo from the hospital.'

'I'll come with you,' said Rachel. 'We'll reconvene later and make a plan. We need to stick together, albeit not literally as we can't leave the house empty,' she added, chewing her lip in anguish.

I noticed that she wasn't limping anymore but she had a red rash covering her neck and shoulders, just like the one she always got after managerial meetings or when Matron turned up unannounced on the ward. Stress!

The atmosphere was tense to say the least, it reflected our anxious moods. The whole sequence of events was creepy. No one had actually come out with it yet but I sensed that we were all thinking along the same lines. Someone was trying to scare us and they must have been in the house. That prospect was deeply disturbing. The thought that someone may have been in the house whilst we were out was bad enough, touching our personal belongings, etc. But the thought that someone had been here with us, nearby, watching our every move was terrifying.

We decided between us that Amy and Emma would house sit whilst Karen, myself and Jill went to the village shop for some milk and maybe some snooping. We wanted to find out if the story about a man dying in the house was fact or fiction and what better way to find out than by asking the locals.

'Be careful and stay together,' I said to Amy as we left.

'Same goes for you,' replied Emma.

'Get a soap on a rope, if possible, or a bar of soap will suffice,' ordered Amy rubbing her hands together. I could almost hear her mind ticking over.

# CHAPTER 13

We decided to take the scenic route via the public footpath.

It was downhill through a wooded glade that led into a meadow with the village beyond. Jill and I looked down at our feet together. We had open-toed sandals on. 'Highly inappropriate footwear,' mocked Karen, marching past in brown lace-ups. She also had a backpack, a bottle of water, and was wearing her blue, floppy sun hat. Her new binoculars hanging around her neck completed the explorer look. She was taking things very seriously by the looks of it and good for her.

There was definitely no time to change our shoes, we decided, as we watched Karen disappear over the stile.

'You've forgotten your hiking poles,' I shouted.

'There's no rush,' said Jill. 'Let her get on. Hopefully, she'll wait for us at the bottom.'

It was a glorious day again, in stark contrast to the nighttime weather. The sun was high, blazing brightly in a sea of blue, not a cloud in sight. What a change we encountered on the other side of the stile.

The footpath led us through a wooded valley. There was no sign of Karen, nor anyone else. It was magical. The birdsong had vanished, replaced by the gentle babbling of the brook which weaved around the ancient tree roots beside us.

'Ooh, look at all that moss,' cooed Jill. 'It'd be fantastic in my hanging baskets,' she muttered.

It was enchanting and my mind happily wandered. The sun beamed through at different angles, highlighting everything in its path. It was as if you could see the air as the mist and dust lit up around us. Hundreds of orb spider webs were strung between the branches, their silk glistening with tiny jewels of dew. I shuddered momentarily as the image of the spider in the house flashed before me, forever imprinted on my mind.

The lace flies and midges became fairies in my imaginary world. Every shade of green immersed us as the sun's rays dappled the flora and fauna claiming everything it possibly could. A glint of fluorescent blue caught my eye as the damselflies, like tiny sapphires, broke up the emerald scenery just for an instant. We lapped up nature's display, our fantasies chasing cares and worries away. It was the most relaxed I had felt all weekend.

It was easy-going on our feet as it was all downhill. Every now and then a gentle breeze would waft past us, cooling our faces and fluttering the leaves. I thought about that icy chill in the hallway, then whisked it away not wanting to spoil my enchantment. I could see Jill was relaxed and enjoying herself as she snapped memories of these beautiful scenes. Shame Karen had not taken time to enjoy it.

The path had widened, the stream as well. The trees looked older now, their roots lay bare as the earth exposed them. The lower branches, though living, lay on the ground as if resting, tired from their longevity. Moss had covered them for protection like nature's blanket. The sun yonder allowed their trunks to show their strength as their silhouettes towered skyward as they had done for centuries.

The flora that survived here was stunning, every fern you could imagine. Thousands of delicate fronds, now unfurled, surrounded us exposing their intricacy. There were some small bell-shaped flowers on the edge of the stream. We both stopped to admire them. Initially, I thought it was wild garlic but on closer inspection, it wasn't. There was no pungent smell. The tiny white flowers scattered over the bank, making a lacy edging outlining the water's winding path. I took a photograph, as did Jill, and I made a mental note to search for it in my wildflower book. It was pennycress, I reckoned.

We didn't need a path to guide us through this magnificent hollow. The golden sunlight blazed brightly where the woodland ended. The sun was blinding as we emerged into the meadow. We expected to see Karen but there was no sign of her.

'I expect she is at the shop by now,' laughed Jill.

We hurried through the meadow, deciding that the uphill stroll back would allow time to admire the flowers.

We soon found the village shop which doubled as a Post Office and we expected to see Karen inside. The first person we noticed was a cantankerous looking old man wearing a string vest. Oh, and trousers of course! They were tweed turn-ups and the fly was enormous, groin to chest. He was sitting precariously on an ancient wooden chair which seemed to be propped up by his walking stick. Jill sauntered over, humming, as she admired his knick-knacks.

'Breakages must be paid for,' read the sign. I nudged Jill reminding her of her very wise words. Look but don't touch. I knew by the way she was lingering that she was building up to something. She peered down at his swollen feet then knelt beside him rubbing her ankle.

'Excuse me,' she said politely, tapping his knee. He was startled and not overly pleased.

'£4.99,' he shouted, 'and you could do with a bigger size.' We realised he was looking at her sandals.

'Oh no, sir! These are mine. My ankle is rather swollen and I wondered if you knew an easier route back to where we're staying?'

He fiddled with his hearing aid whilst I tried to drag her away. 'I'm staying up on the hill,' she continued, 'in one of the Victorian houses there. Windy Passage. Do you know it?'

'Pills? No, we don't! We're not a chemist. And the nearest toilets are in the car park across the road.'

I noticed someone, whom I presumed was his wife, eavesdropping from behind the counter. She had heard the house name, as did everyone else in the shop. Jill had said it loud and clear.

The woman beckoned us over, I could almost make out her ears twitching.

'Holidaymakers, are you?' she asked, peering over the top of her glasses.

'A ladies weekend break,' I answered, accidentally emphasising the word 'ladies'. 'I don't suppose you sell ant powder, only the house is overrun with creepy crawlies.' Initially, she clammed up but as soon as the other customers exited the shop the gossip demon possessed her.

'I would imagine it is a sad, dreary house my dear after what happened there. That poor man. He was a musician, I believe, and his lady friend. Both talented by all accounts. Sometimes we could hear the music, guitar mostly, if the wind was blowing the right way. Must have been noisy for the neighbours. He didn't stand a chance on those old, steep stairs. Such a shame! They hadn't lived there long, rented it off a foreigner who lives in London. Mind you, I often wonder why he tripped and fell. A bit suspicious, if you ask me. There was a lot of gossip in the village for weeks after, which I didn't like. I've not got time for gossip. Perhaps something startled him. They say he'd had a lot to drink.'

We didn't need to prompt or ask any questions, we couldn't get a word in edgeways. The story had been confirmed.

'Oh, by the way, we've lost our friend.' Before I could give any details, she'd answered.

'There was a single woman here about twenty minutes ago. Fortyish, slim, nice blue hat and funny, brown shoes. Made me smile,' she chuckled. 'She bought the last of the strawberries and some clotted cream. Wanted to know the quickest route back. Anyone would think she was in a race!'

It was definitely Karen. 'Forty-ish,' she will be pleased.

'Oh and do you sell soap and air freshener?' asked Jill.

The sun was at its peak as we started the uphill journey back.

'Phew!' puffed Jill, fanning herself. 'We should have bought some water.'

It wasn't long before we needed to stop and catch our breath. It was, indeed, a steep ascent. We gazed around admiring the beauty of the English countryside. The view of the sea was magnificent. Its turquoise shimmer was subtle, the stillness serene. There was no sound of the waves, only the birds broke the silence.

About halfway up the field, I heard a gentle hum in the distance and I noticed a row of hives on the slope at the other side of the meadow. Jill had noticed too, we smiled and both said together, 'We should've bought some of that local honey from the shop.'

We strolled onward through the tapestry of colour. The grasses wafted gently in the breeze, swaying the flowers in a colourful carnival dance. A plume of red petals erupted from the poppies like fireworks as a bumblebee laden with pollen stripped them naked. Their few hours of glory cut short. Its flight was precarious, defying nature, as it carried its huge yellow baskets. It drowned out the honey bees as it buzzed away. The array of flowers was fabulous. Ox-eye daisies domineering in patches, their yellow centres like sprinkled sunbeams. The sun's rays reflected on the buttercups turning the whole field gold.

'My favourites are the cornflowers,' murmured Jill bending down to snap a close-up.

I beckoned her over. On the edge of the path was a cluster of bee orchids which I knew were rare. The pink patch completed the rainbow and we added them to our album, capturing the beautiful bee markings adorning these masters of disguise. The thought of the cool, dark woodland spurred us on as it was a long, hard trek in the sweltering heat. When we eventually got there, the wooded glade didn't disappoint. The cool air hit us like air conditioning. We splashed our faces with the running water from the stream, a joyous yet simple pleasure.

With renewed vigour, we continued our ascent. Eventually, we were greeted by dappled sunlight shining on the small patch of grass in front of the stile. Our exit was grand as well. Wild foxgloves stood tall in groups; their fuschia pink enticing the bees to delve into the nectar-laden funnels. Deadly digitalis, a beauty in disguise.

Nature's apothecary surrounded us with its variety of plants and flowers providing both healing remedies and poisons. I noticed a death cap in the shade by the side of a rotting tree stump. 'Highly toxic,' I whispered subconsciously and the memory of the mushroom stroganoff suddenly took on a new, much darker meaning.

As we approached the house, we could see the front door was open and there was quite a commotion inside. They signalled to us to hurry up and we were virtually dragged through the door. Rachel and Liz had returned with Mo who was following the doctor's orders and resting upstairs. By the looks of it, Karen had not returned.

I realised the door had been open to disperse the horrendous smell in the hallway but it was the upheaval that took me aback and took my mind off Karen. They had taken the stair runner up, a wrench lay redundant. The floorboard beneath had already been loosened. It was lifted with ease.

'Hold your nose,' Liz warned.

Emma was retching in a dramatic fashion. Under the floorboard lay a grisly sight. The fetid, rotting carcass of some poor animal. It was obvious to all that no such creature could have found its own way there. Someone had made it an early grave. Amy had decided it was probably a fox or cat due to the tail length. There wasn't much left to go on. It was crawling with maggots, the remaining rotting flesh was a grey-black slime. Putrid. The bones lay exposed before us as we choked on the rancid smell.

'We waited so you could see it,' announced Rachel, wearing marigolds and passing a bin bag to Amy. 'We've all had gloves on,' she added.

'Hang on!' I said. 'It needs to stay exactly where it is, undisturbed. The way things are going this could end up as a crime scene.'

'Amy! Take the bin bag and get the seagull out of the bin, we need to keep that as well,' I added in an authoritative voice that I didn't recognise.

The floorboards under the carpet told a sinister story. We knew what the faded, brown stain was. A fingerprint of a lost life. We were all quiet, the power and realisation of the tragedy that had occurred at this very spot resonated around us. The air had turned ice-cold yet there was no wind.

Emotion overcame me. I was shivering and my eyes watered as an immense feeling of sadness enveloped me. We carefully put everything back in place in silence.

'We can put up with the smell for one more night,' said Rachel quietly.

# CHAPTER 14

Mo appeared at the top of the stairs, understandably considering what was going on at the bottom of them.

'Be careful!' warned Jill, rushing to assist her.

'Get off,' she laughed. 'I'm fine, honestly. I fancy a nice cup of tea.'

'I'm on it,' chirped Emma, giving her the thumbs up.

Amy and I dragged the easy chair over to the window so she could sit comfortably with her feet up and enjoy the wonderful view. Rachel and Liz had already filled her in about the seagull on the journey back from the hospital. Mo had not mentioned anything about seeing someone at the top of the stairs and they hadn't broached the subject. I wondered for a minute whether my recollection of events at the hospital were correct.

I plotted my interrogation whilst they ensured she was relaxed and comfortable. Emma poured her tea from a proper teapot, a treat in itself, and she'd found a bone china cup and saucer at the back of the cupboard. Fit for a queen.

'Do you remember telling me that you saw someone at the top of the stairs?' I asked with far too much excitement.

They all closed in wanting to hear it straight from the horse's mouth. Their manner was overbearing which made me think better of my brash exuberance. I fetched her the last two homemade cookies to loosen her tongue and we all gathered around. Mo looked surprised by the question and I wondered if the head injury had caused amnesia or if she had actually said it at all.

'Shut your eyes and try and remember,' I coaxed. Time ticked by as she devoured the biscuits. Patience was not my best virtue and my obvious lack of it prompted a tut from Amy.

'Are you sitting comfortably?' Mo teased, eking it out. She looked like she was thinking hard as she gazed out the window. The room was silent apart from a solitary, extraordinarily long bowel sound. Amy wrapped her arms around her stomach in protest to gag the rude interruption.

'Think!' prompted Liz. Her tone was rude and impatient but it provided the impetus Mo needed.

And so she began.


'My memory is patchy so please bear with me. I was returning from the bathroom, somewhat inebriated, when a strong smell of aftershave caught in my throat, almost making me gag. It overpowered the usual horrid smell, that's why I remember it so clearly. I turned to where the smell was coming from and that's when I saw it.'

'It?!' queried Rachel, loudly.

Mo hesitated and then continued…

'The apparition appeared, just for an instant. My vision was blurred, the light was dim and flickering. The fuzzy outline I saw was the figure of a man, I think.'

She held back again, cautiously, as she tried to relive the memory.

'It was all one shade, pale and misty, yet almost translucent. It could have been a woman as the whole thing was billowing, like a long dress flowing, perhaps? Suddenly, a red haze engulfed me and I was falling into a deep, dark abyss. The next thing I remember was a sharp pain in my ear lobe,' she said, looking at me accusingly.

'Apparition!' hissed Amy as she questioned the narrative with suspicion and scepticism. She wouldn't be able to do her job if she believed in ghosts so she was having none of it. Mo's reply was curt and final.

'The state I was in...that's how I perceived it. I remember the primal fear before I blacked out.'

She stared out of the window, her pensive mood was reflected on her face. We were all gobsmacked. Amy had left the room in displeasure and disbelief.

'More tea?' I asked in a light, happy tone which I feigned.

Karen had still not returned. Mo was the lookout and every now and then someone else would scan the horizon or open the front door to check up and down the hill. Liz had rung her mobile several times and it was going straight to the answerphone. I checked my watch again and decided if she hadn't returned in the next ten minutes that I would look for her with Amy. I peered out the window towards the stile hoping she'd appear.

My eyes, however, were drawn in the other direction. Something was moving just below the top of the hedge across the road. I squinted. The sun was bright but I could just make it out. It was Karen's hat. It moved a few inches, then stopped, then edged further along.

'What's going on?' asked Amy as she stood alongside me.

I beckoned the others over in haste, making sure my eyes never left sight of the hat. We all stood in silence captivated as the blue material, seemingly with a life of its own, edged along before settling out of sight.

'Something's amiss,' said Jill. 'It's definitely Karen. I can just see her backpack.'

'Hold your ground,' cautioned Amy. 'She's trying to signal us. If we're lucky, she might use sign language.'

'Not if she doesn't want to be seen,' drawled Rachel.

'Shall I ring her?' asked Emma.

'No, that might give her away! She obviously doesn't want those creepy neighbours to see her coming in here,' piped up Mo. 'We need a diversion to ensure whoever is watching looks out the back, not the front.'

'Bikini time then?' suggested Amy. 'I'm convinced there's a pervert next door after the scare in the hot tub the other night. Speaking of which, a man came and cleaned it this morning and he wasn't best pleased. We're not to go in with make-up or sunscreen on. Apparently, the water had the worst case of scum he'd ever seen. He virtually accused us of purposely tampering with it by adding dirt or grease and the PH was totally off the scale. Why on earth would we do that? And I'm pretty sure he read my mind as my sneer was as vicious as it was condescending.'

'Lucky he didn't test the alcohol percentage, it would've been at least 50% proof,' laughed Jill.

Emma put the music on and opened the back windows. Liz brought out a tray of fake piña coladas with all the trimmings but minus the alcohol. We'd all made a collective decision to make it a 'dry Sunday' as we needed our wits about us and our livers could do with the rest.

Jill remained on the lookout at the front and would signal Karen when we judged it was safe to come in. Today we wanted to entice a Peeping Tom!

The tub bubbled, the music played, and our laughter came easily. We were soon high on fruit juice and atmosphere. With minimal effort I rambled on, keeping my voice low apart from loudly emphasising the word 'SEX' which I made sure was in at least every other sentence. Amy was best placed to detect movement from next door's windows and I was fixed on the bird hide.

Our sunglasses gave us a covert advantage by keeping the direction of our glances secret, a trick I had learnt from Roy on beach holidays in the Mediterranean. I spotted a glint in the bird hide and then hasty, shadowy movements convinced me that the watcher was there. I whispered to Emma whilst discreetly pointing my melon in the perpetrator's direction.

She gave an Oscar-winning performance. Though her bikini was already high-legged, a quick wedgie achieved an X-rated effect. Aided by buoyancy, she ended up kneeling on the seating shelf with her ass in all of its glory pointing directly at the bird hide as she seductively sipped her cocktail. My cleavage ensured that attention was well and truly diverted in our direction.

We all heard something drop in the hide and we knew we'd struck gold.

Amy gave the signal and the others ushered Karen in through the front door.

She was quite bedraggled and out of breath, but managed to unload the scone ingredients and the now extra, extra clotted cream before she did anything else. Rachel ordered her to sit down as we rushed in to dry off and change our clothes. Liz had made her an Earl Grey tea with two heaped teaspoons of sugar as she could see she was visibly shaken.

'Where have you been?' asked Jill. 'We were really worried.'

'Did you get lost?' said Amy squinting.

'Certainly not!' Karen snapped, her feistiness returning. 'I decided to take the road route back as I was almost eaten alive in that dismal jungle. It was heaving with midges,' she grumbled, scratching the gnat bites which were appearing by the minute up both of her legs. It looked like a prickly heat rash had got the better of her arms and neck.

'Not been eating enough Marmite?' questioned Amy. Her tone was friendly now, presumably mercy had been granted as she eyed the red hives with sympathy.

'I would've been back ages ago if it wasn't for my strange encounter.'

'Well, go on!' urged Liz.

Karen recounted her story, reliving the drama and revelling in the attention. 'The road route seemed to be a lot further so I hopped over a stile and followed a footpath through a copse which I could see was leading to a small common. Though my sense of direction is excellent, one must make use of technology so I summoned the compass on my phone. It wasn't long before I heard raised voices up ahead whilst I was still in the trees, so I edged a bit closer and spied through a hole in the hawthorn. They were sitting on a bench. An argument was in process. I was in a prime position to witness events but just out of earshot so I was unable to make out all of what they were saying. I soon realised it was our peculiar neighbours so I kept my whereabouts hidden. They were arguing and it looked as though he was trying to persuade her to do something that she didn't agree with.'

'What did he look like?' I asked, curiosity making me butt in. After all, none of us had actually seen him. Her smile gave the answer away and she blurted it out with excitement.

'Average height, I suppose. His hair was black and shiny. The white t-shirt enhanced his olive skin and emphasised his biceps. He had tight jeans on and his bum...Well, he reminded me of Gino off the telly,' she gasped.

'Oooh,' drawled Mo. 'Go on!'

'Italian accent as well,' she added with a quivering voice which sent Jill in a spin to fetch cold water.

'Well I never,' said Rachel. 'I wouldn't have imagined him to look like that!'

'Worth getting the bikini out then,' smiled Emma.

'Well, she's a pretty woman,' I reminded them, before cringing at my shallow words.

'Hurry up,' pleaded Amy, sounding bored and uninterested.

Karen continued.

'Their body language was confusing. I'm pretty sure they were arguing as I saw him forcefully grab her arm and she pulled away but then it was like her body and spirit melted and she pulled him close. They were standing intimately by now. The embrace was raw with passion, as was the frenzied kiss that followed.' Karen paused and her eyes seemed to almost glaze over with the memory.

I nudged her and urged her to continue amid increasing tuts from Amy.

'The heated desire was catching as it caused the worst menopausal flush I've ever had,' she recalled, gulping the cold water. 'I fanned my face with my hat and knocked a huge furry caterpillar down my cleavage. I just managed to stifle a scream as he led her hurriedly through the trees. I could see the steam rising behind them.'

'Mist or heat haze from the forest floor?' snarled Amy.

'They went uphill towards the house, it must've been a shortcut.'

'What a foolish woman!' cursed Amy. I wondered whether she meant Karen or the neighbour.

'Well, we don't know what goes on behind closed doors. Domestic abuse of all types can happen in all walks of life,' added Rachel, 'and individuals react in different ways.'

'She looked extremely happy after that kiss,' added Karen. 'I think initially she was disagreeing with him but he broke her down and she gave in. Mind you, I'd be tempted,' she added feverishly, provoking a dirty look from Liz. 'I'd say whatever he's planning, she's in on it.'

I suggested we take a break for lunch. After all, there was a lot to take in.

We decided on cheese and crackers as we hadn't even opened the cheeses yet. We all rallied around at the thought of food. All this drama meant that appetites were even more ravenous than usual. I set about laying the table, grateful for a menial task as my imagination was working at full throttle.

A rustic breadboard made for the perfect vessel. It was soon laden with a magnificent assortment. Vintage cave cheddar, garlic roule, camembert, Roquefort and stilton. The board was soon overflowing so Amy took a stance and, rightly so, stated that we shouldn't open anything else.

Grapes, olives, piccolo tomatoes, chutneys and pickles completed the line-up. Karen was trying all the different crackers, spreading them thickly with the best farmhouse butter.

'I don't eat much cheese,' she stated. Her arteries seemed to bulge from her neck in protest at the fib. It was partly true. She didn't eat as much cheese as she did butter.

We all tucked in but agreed it was not quite the same without a glass of wine. Willpower weakened and Amy soon appeared with a bottle of merlot and chardonnay.

'One glass each,' she instructed.

'Not for me,' said Mo.

'Me neither,' added Jill.

I could almost see the haloes forming and guilt set in momentarily.

'Just one glass each,' Rachel reiterated seriously.

I noticed Amy craftily fetching two large wine glasses for us both. I decided not to point it out. The guilt had vanished, replaced with desire. We gave Mo the rundown of the morning's discussion before showing her the list of things that we needed to discuss.

'Feel free to add anything,' I encouraged, dreading what else might come to light.

'Well we've confirmed the story about a man dying in the house,' I began, quickly filling Karen in on what we'd found out at the Post Office.

'I definitely saw a figure or a vision of someone at the top of the stairs,' said Mo.

'We've solved the horrendous smell,' added Rachel. 'You missed all that, Karen.'

'Well, the hallway still stinks,' Karen complained before Rachel filled her in with the gory details.

'You have been busy,' Karen smiled, sipping her wine and eating the last of the butter.

I continued methodically. 'The spider was here Friday night so it seems likely that the house had been set up before our arrival. Someone must have entered the house when we were out Saturday to plant the creepy crawlies but worse still is the fact that he somehow got in while we were here and managed to frighten Mo half to death! I say 'he' as she smelt aftershave, remember? By the way, Roy has replied to my text. I asked him about the red eyes we've seen. He reckons it could be old-fashioned night-vision goggles without cups shielding the wearer's eyes. That would allow the infrared to be seen. He says it's very amateurish and defeats the object unless for some reason you wanted someone to see weird, red eyes. I didn't go into further details as he would have made us come home.'

'Right,' sighed Liz. 'We need to figure out how he's getting in. He could have a key, of course.'

Before she could finish, Mo stepped in, 'I noticed the loft hatch slightly open on Saturday afternoon.'

'So did I,' stammered Rachel, standing up.

'I've heard movements in the loft,' I added. 'Thinking about it, it sounded just like footsteps.'

We all shuddered together and downed the last of the wine.

'No more alcohol,' stated Karen. 'We need to make a plan.'


I stood up to ensure their attention was focused as I wanted them to hear my latest brainwave.

'If he was in the house yesterday he could have spiked our drinks or food or both. The walk this morning through the woods and fields gave me the idea. I saw lots of wild herbs and poisonous plants. Perhaps he likes a bit of foraging?'

We had all experienced unusual symptoms and we knew that hallucinations weren't common with alcohol alone. The same stark realisation hit us all. It was all getting far too dark. My head was spinning. I focused on Liz who was also a qualified aromatherapist.

'We need a herbal remedy to make a potion. We cast a spell and whisk all this torment away,' I chanted trying to lighten the mood.

'If only we were real witches,' winked Rachel with a wicked smile.

# CHAPTER 15

We decided that we needed to test the theory that someone was entering the house via the loft. Rachel retrieved her on-call kit from the car which included a torch on a headband. You can use your imagination to figure out what it was usually used for.

'There must be a loft ladder,' said Liz, staring up at the hatch which was at quite a height due to the high ceilings.

'This is crazy,' cursed Amy as she dragged a chair from the bedroom.

Rachel's practicality was already in progress as she rummaged through the airing cupboard.

'Good idea,' murmured Amy. She was excited now as she was an expert at unravelling white sheets. This time she got to tie them together, or so she thought as she fought with the pile that was slowly smothering her.

'I'm looking for a pole,' mumbled Rachel, deep in thought.

'Abracadabra!' I proclaimed, producing a long cane as if it were a magic wand.

'Where did you find that?' she replied.

I pointed. 'Hooked on the wall in the corner.'

She pushed open the hatch as she delicately knelt on the chair. We could see quite clearly a large, rusty metal loop just inside the square, dark opening. With great tenacity, she gently pulled and slowly but surely the ancient loft ladder creaked towards us. Karen was giddy with anticipation. Her hands were shaking as she videoed the unfolding stairway on her phone. Amy had changed into joggers and had the torch ready to ascend into the darkness. I climbed up the steps behind her with Karen on my tail.

'One at a time,' urged Liz. 'It looks really old and it might not take the weight.'

'We're only light,' I argued, knowing full well that our actions were foolhardy as the ladder looked flimsy and rusted.

They gathered around below us, peering upwards. Emma had taken over the filming but fought to steady her hand. Nerves had got the better of some of us. I moved alongside Amy, unable to contain my excitement.

'What can you see?' whispered Karen who was just below us. Liz was gripping her shirt to prevent her from climbing further. Surely the ladder wouldn't hold three!

The space inside was huge. The roof towered above us. The old trusses were dotted with woodworm and covered in dense cobwebs. The sight of them made me cringe. Amy was shining the torch as we couldn't see a light switch. As the torch was on her head, its direction was haphazard to say the least until we forced her to remove it. The loft was cluttered with old furniture and pictures draped in moth-eaten dust sheets. The smell of damp lingered and mould crept out from the corners like lichen. The torch beam caught the dust motes and we nearly screamed as a bat swept across the rafters to the gable end. Amy lost grip of the torch so I grabbed it, putting my fingers to my lips as muffled movements came from next door.

I directed the torchlight onto the adjoining wall where a flimsy shelf unit resided. We both agreed that there was a square-shaped outline of a bodged-up opening behind it. A crude attempt to camouflage the opening was glaringly apparent. As I dipped the beam downwards, our suspicions were confirmed. Just as well we hadn't set foot in the loft as we may have missed what was now blatantly obvious from eye level. The footprints in the dust led diagonally across the floorboards to the shelf unit.

Amy retreated. I knew she was scared and that resonated in me. I was terrified. Karen's head popped up beside me, reassuring us momentarily. She gasped in horror. The noises next door were getting louder, as were our heartbeats. I glanced to my right and saw the shape of a guitar protruding from behind a dust sheet. I just managed to pull an old sheet of music through the dust before the others dragged us down. I handed the music to Amy. It was watermarked and matted together with thick cobwebs. Jill put her hand over Liz's mouth to stifle the scream as a spider dropped out and raced over her foot.

'That's tiny,' mocked Emma, dropping her phone and retreating to her room.

Rachel wound up the rickety ladder with expertise and closed the loft in haste.

'Well, what's up there?' asked Mo.

We reconvened in the master bedroom. Its heady heights notched the view up another level. It was stupendous. We could just about make out the top of the lighthouse and Lundy Island which was either hidden in the heat haze or shrouded in mist. White specks of surf dabbed the ocean and a handful of yachts sliced through the waves on the horizon. Between us we gave them the rundown on the loft, each taking it in turns to speak.

'So that's it,' said Liz. 'That's his route. God knows what he's planning tonight. Maybe it's all a game? A bit of weekend fun? It could all be over now if she's talked him down.'

'I don't think so,' piped up Karen. 'From what I witnessed earlier, he's got other devious ideas. The way they were arguing suggests it's bad. I think the worst is yet to come. She was trying to persuade him against it. I'm sure of it.'

'But what could be the motive?' Jill queried. 'Why try to ruin our weekend escape by scaring us half to death?'

'And that's exactly what's happening,' said Mo.

'Who would want to stay in a haunted house and who would want to buy one?' asked Emma. 'Maybe they are trying to give the house a bad reputation so they can buy it cheaply?'

'Now that's feasible,' agreed Jill.

'The worst case scenario is they are a pair of sadistic psychopaths and they actually intend to cause us physical harm. Remember a man supposedly, accidentally, fell to his death in this very house.' I gulped. 'Sorry to look on the bad side,' I added sheepishly.

'I suggest we think it over and make a plan before anything kicks off tonight,' said Rachel in a totally pissed off voice.

'We need sustenance,' trumped Karen. 'I'll make some scones and we'll hold a discussion.'

After a quick forty winks, Karen began making the scones with Rachel as her kitchen assistant. The nap had recharged our batteries and lightened our moods. Hopefully, we could think straight and do the sensible thing but sensible was not in my vocabulary.

'Can you rinse the strawberries, Karen?' asked Rachel, politely.

'Yum! Homemade jam,' cooed Amy. Rachel slipped her a wooden spoon before Karen turned around.

'Jam! For God's sake! I've not got time to make jam with all that's going on! The strawberries are an accompaniment or garnish.'

We all knew Amy hated jam, Karen must've forgotten.

'Oh dear, the butter is all gone!' Amy said with playful spite as she nosed in the fridge.

'And all the wine!' I reminded her, wiping the grin off her face.

'Stop it!' said Mo. 'We've got plans to make! I thought you were interested in those music sheets Amy?' With that, she handed her the musty music sheets. Amy went to find her reading glasses and then settled at the table to study the notes. She very rarely concentrated on anything, couldn't keep still long enough.

'If only I'd brought my keyboard,' she muttered.

The muttering continued and I could see she was getting quite animated.

'I think this is a work in progress. An original song.'

Her voice was loud now and we were all paying attention. The idea that sprang into my mind made me leap up with excitement.

'I've got a brilliant idea,' I stammered rushing to find my phone.

I sent a message to Roy and added that there would be photographs to follow. I ended it with a love heart and a fingers crossed emoji. He was progressing well learning the guitar and his fingerpicking was particularly good. I was hoping that if he could make out the music he might be able to play it.

What if it was the song I kept hearing in the night? A few of us had mentioned the beautiful guitar music and the fact that it was the same melody each time. I felt giddy and frightened at the same time. The butterflies in my stomach were getting stronger by the minute.

By the time I had returned to the kitchen, Amy had deciphered the damaged music and the notes were scrawled down on paper. I photographed her handiwork along with the original music sheets and sent it to Roy. The bloke next door must be playing the guitar, my sensible self assured me. The real me, my crazed self, shortly took over. The fantasy my imagination was weaving was much more powerful and I knew it was also what I was wishing for. Something almost tangible was leading me on to delve into the realms of new possibilities beyond my imagination. I'd been there before. That feeling took me back to a memory that I had long since forgotten...

It was a cold November evening about thirty years ago. I was at the beginning of my nurse training and based at the old General Hospital in the city of Bristol. Basic nursing care was the foundation of training and invariably involved care of the elderly so I was working on one of the many geriatric wards. I'd spent the whole of the late shift holding the hand of an elderly lady who was in the last hours of her life. She was a stoic woman and full of character, though dementia had gripped her quite cruelly. Staff had named her 'Mammy' which she loved as she had no children of her own but had worked most of her life as a nursery nurse.

She would spend most of her time pacing the ward, on good days, cradling and rocking a make-believe baby, gently humming a lullaby to soothe her imaginary babe to sleep. I can still recall the tune now. She maintained her femininity by wearing long, flowery dresses with the same worn-out, lace-up boots. I remembered her face. Her bone structure was strikingly beautiful as was her figure. She had high cheekbones and a long aquiline nose. Her eyes were the palest blue, framed by soft grey waist-length hair which she always wore in a plaited bun.

She had no living family or friends. I was honoured to spend time with her, ensuring she wouldn't die alone. Her passing was peaceful and I knew she didn't suffer. Though I felt a deep sadness, I finished my shift with pride and a warm, content feeling knowing my quiet presence had really mattered.

The wind was howling and a crisp, cruel frost was just appearing as I stepped out into the winter's night. I hurried across the quadrant, pulling my thick, woollen cape tightly around me. I remember the bitterness of the wind and the fear I felt when I got to the subway which led underground to the nurses' home. There were strange shapes and shadows all around on this particular night and the howl of the wind was ghostly.

The subway was a frightening prospect at the best of times. I hesitated, as usual, whilst I plucked up the courage to rush through. The street lamp at the other end urged me on with its gentle glow but the sight of a woman standing beneath the lamp made me move. I was worried about her. Who in their right mind would bring a baby out, even well wrapped in a pram, on a night like this?

As I got nearer, instead of becoming clearer, the figure blurred but the familiarity spurred me on. The long, flowery dress, the distinctive pose, the beautiful bone structure. The shape of the pram was peculiar, unique, old-fashioned. Mist seemed to close in all around like a thick fog as I emerged from the subway. I was astonished as I reached the lamp to find that no one was there and the fear inside me had vanished, it was the overwhelming feeling of self-worth that I cherished the most.

'Julia! Are you with the living?' Liz said as she shook my arm.

'I've been thinking about what you said earlier about foraging and medicinal remedies and POISONS,' she emphasised loudly. She had well and truly captured my attention. I snapped out of my poignant daydream.

The scones were in the oven and the smell in the room was heavenly. I'd found my pocket wildflower book which I hoped would be useful. Liz had settled herself at the table with her pen and notebook and was listing the food we'd eaten on Saturday evening. She scrolled through her phone making notes.

'Did you chop the thyme and parsley up last minute Karen or was it prepared in advance?'

'Last minute,' she answered. 'The flavours are fresher.'

'I'm just mulling it over. If we inadvertently ate some rogue ingredient it had to have been disguised.'

'Mind you, we had all had a lot to drink. Do you think we'd have noticed?' I interjected.

'Well, I would!' snapped Karen before her confidence waned when I reminded her about the essential ingredient she missed out of the nut roast last year.

'I think it was the mushrooms,' said Mo.

'I agree,' piped up Amy. 'I could've done a better job if you'd asked. Some were still whole.'

'That's the point, it gives variety and texture,' added Karen, refusing to be drawn in any further.

'Psilocybe cubensis,' Liz read out slowly. 'Commonly called...shrooms! FUCK! I reckon we had a magic mushroom stroganoff.' I'm convinced the almighty sigh that came from us all was strong enough to create a vortex which caused Karen to drop a plate that then splintered across the floor.

We all closed in around the picture displayed on Liz's phone. We knew the food bin would be virtually empty as food, like alcohol, never got wasted. Before anyone else spoke, Amy was halfway to the caddy to search for the incriminating mushroom that Mo had left. We all remembered it as Mo had said it looked odd.

'It looks suspect,' said Karen, poking it around on the chopping board. 'I can't be certain as there was quite a variety. It can go in a food bag as evidence, as I think that's the way this whole saga is heading.'

'Scones are done!' called Rachel. She knew Karen would want to check so she busied herself making the tea. The smell was mouthwatering. We all grabbed a plate and sat like lapdogs at the table. We knew we wouldn't last until they were completely cool. Our quandary was completely forgotten as we buttered the warm scones, spooned on the best strawberry jam and dolloped thick, clotted cream on the top.

Several of us put the cream on before the jam, which sparked a friendly debate that, given the circumstances, was most welcome.

# CHAPTER 16

I finished my tea whilst sitting on the window seat alongside Mo. The sun streamed in through the window warming our faces. The room was blissfully quiet as we all languished in our own thoughts.

The afternoon lull was soothing, the sunlight making light of our predicament, but I felt we'd been led into a transient false sense of security. The longer I sat thinking, the more worried I became. My confidence was diminishing.

It was Mo, the oldest and probably the wisest, who spoke first. Perhaps she sensed the doubts as she glanced around the room, noticing, like myself, the cracks in the wall and ceiling and the cobwebs. There was definitely a web-weaving spider somewhere.

'Do you think we've made the right decision in staying here to face the consequences? We have other options. We could speak to the police!'

'Or we could go next door and introduce ourselves to the neighbours,' suggested Rachel.

'We could be in great danger,' added Emma as she filed her toenails.

Amy was doing pilates and to make things worse she was wearing leggings. Sensing the stares, she was quick to bite back. 'They're jeggings,' she snapped before anyone dared open their mouths. No one uttered a word. There was silence for a good ten minutes as we all grappled with our thoughts. Not about Amy's jeggings, but about what was occurring in this strange house and what we were getting ourselves into. Had we finally bitten off more than we could chew?

Our collective feistiness took me back to the horrendous all-day interview that some of us had endured to be selected for the midwifery course. You used to be able to do an eighteen-month course if you were already a qualified nurse but it was particularly difficult to get chosen as there weren't many places. The mere memory made me alter my posture. I sat bolt upright.

I would never forget the stress and preparation for that one day of terror and humiliation to prove that out of 400 shortlisted applicants you were good enough and strong enough to be a woman's advocate. The practical skills could be learned, the studying was an essential commitment, but the character and personality of the candidate was the core of what they craved. Degrees and academia were just the icing on the cake. Life experience, certain personality traits, and a hard-working ethos were the qualities that they coveted and they had eight hours to find them. So, they worked you hard.

Surely if I could succeed there, I could tackle whatever was going on in this house and I wouldn't be doing this alone. We had teamwork, camaraderie and friendship on our side and there was no better combination. We needed to form a plan so that when it was nighttime and the strange wind blew, we would be ready to solve the mysterious happenings by catching the perpetrator red-handed.

We would be ready and waiting. I was up for it as I knew we could do it, but the others needed to come to the same conclusion. They were getting there. It was Karen that kickstarted the ball of pent-up fury that we had all kept caged.

'How dare he!' she seethed. She was marching across the room. She looked like she was looking for someone to head butt. 'Our anniversary weekend practically ruined! And by a man!'

'Bastard!' shouted Liz at the adjoining wall.

'Dream on pervert,' snarled Emma, slapping her own ass so hard that she flinched and broke a nail.

The best was yet to come...

Amy had slipped out of the room. She had returned with a vengeance, a pillowcase and a bar of soap. She'd worked herself up and was shaking with anger, which hampered her efforts. She put the soap inside the pillowcase and proceeded to violently twist and spin it. Her actions reminded me of her tomfoolery in the empty clinic corridor when she'd expertly swung a mop bucket full of water around and up over her head to prove a point. She never spilt a drop which was a bit like her wine glass.

That wouldn't be the case today as she lost her grip and the pillowcase flew across the room, shattering the vase on the table. Glass splinters scattered and water seeped across the table like an omen. The sound was ear-piercing and brought us back to the reality of what we were facing. It gave us the impetus we needed and an hour later we had a plan in place.

Emma would be on guard by the back door. Jill would be stationed at the front door, ready to phone 999 at the signal. The rest of us would be upstairs watching the loft, ready to pounce.

We laughed as Rachel practised her usual pre-rugby match routine. She stomped around the room grunting obscenities. Meanwhile, Amy was man-handling a bean bag. If she could shear a large sheep single-handedly, she could take on ten men. Speed and the element of surprise stood us in good stead. Woman power!

Jill's role, though not as exciting, was the most important. We all knew from experience that one of the first steps in a crisis was always to call for help. As long as she made the call on cue, and the police arrived as promptly as the ambulance had last night, we just might be alright. It wasn't worth thinking about the worst-case scenario so I didn't and that stopped me from calling the ridiculous escapade off. Something was spurring me on. It was much stronger than confidence. I felt safe. I felt invincible.

I Googled 'magic mushrooms' for the tenth time to check how long they stay in the system. Apparently, effects could last for up to 24 hours, especially in older people...not that we were. Hopefully they weren't dry mushrooms as they were much more potent, especially when mixed with alcohol. And they'd definitely been mixed with alcohol. A lot of alcohol.

We decided to try and enjoy the rest of the day as best we could. That was also a vital part of the plan. Things needed to appear normal to whoever was watching. We wouldn't be drinking but a party atmosphere was essential as we were sure they would rely on us being compromised. After the last two nights' shenanigans, we must look like easy targets. Well someone was in for one hell of a shock!

We suspected it would be late when he made his move. Well, it could be a she. I had not ruled that out. It was usually dark when the strange things happened but we would be waiting. We wouldn't be asleep and we wouldn't be drunk.

This was going to be a night shift on another level!

# CHAPTER 17
## 'Darren'

The loft was his favourite place but his tense posture told another tale.

Rigid like an uncomfortable chair. Stiff as a board, or a corpse. A precursor to the pain that would follow and it did, as always. Face followed body as his jaw became taut and a grimace evolved below his wrinkled brow as the migraine began its crippling course.

Stress and tension. The cause of a multitude of ailments. He stared briefly at the square of blue sky framed by the Velux window but there was no relief. The shaft of sunlight beamed through, piercing the clouds and shedding light on the sordid display on the desk beside him, stoking the pain in his head further.

It was the noise that started the dismal chain of events, he knew that, and the fact that it was out of his control made it worse. But not for much longer. Bitter thoughts heightened his suffering as the chip on his shoulders grew heavier until his whole body ached with self-pity. The empty vodka bottle was a constant reminder of the night before and dented any optimism, well, apart from the thought of another drink.

The loft conversion was his hideaway, a sanctuary, just like the room all those years ago. But there had been no escape from the noise here, as there wasn't then. Now his retirement was plagued by noisy family gatherings, or hen and stag parties, virtually every weekend. It was a rerun of his childhood. The tormenting reminder had caused debilitating flashbacks.

The memory of the booming bass pulsated like the throbbing vein in his head. It would spiral down his core, infecting every nerve, muscle and cell, until he was an irritable, jittering wreck. It was usually his teenage years that came flooding back. His self-harm was to rake over it again and again. The 'ifs' and 'buts' were a menace that never went away, especially when he recognised that he'd had so much potential.

Studying had come naturally to him. He had been a high achiever throughout school and was on course to achieve his goals. He was nearly always top of the class and his reports were full of top grades, praise and commendations. A smile almost formed whenever he remembered the one-upmanship and the fact that his achievements were almost effortless. The gene pool had dealt him an unrivalled academic mind. In his case, nature trumped nurture on every level. There was no debate.

His ambition had been to gain sponsorship to medical school. In those days, without wealthy parents and a certain background and social class, entry was tantamount to impossible. He got into grammar school and was actually on course until his mother took up with that wannabe musician.

That Saturday night flashed back like the pain piercing his temple...

He had returned from a mate's house late evening to finish an assignment. He heard the noise as he turned into the close. The party was in full swing, old bangers and motorbikers littered the pavements outside. It was mayhem inside, well, it looked like armageddon. The lounge resembled a rubbish tip, the only thing missing was the seagulls. Bottles, cans and bodies were strewn everywhere. Someone had tried to light a fire, the burnt paper clearly from his desk. His mother's boyfriend slumped on the top like a hideous Guy Fawkes. The beaten-down settee was dotted with cigarette burns and the candles flickered, reflecting on the tarnished silver spoons now empty. The opium already coursing through knackered veins.

The dining table where he did all his assignments had collapsed, along with all of the strangers surrounding it, but it was the hole in the wall that shocked him the most. That's where his eyes lingered while he took it all in. The crude opening had started from a punch and been ripped apart as some idiot had tried to claw their way through to the kitchen. The tattered, do-it-yourself hatch provided easy access to the alcohol.

He found his mother in the bedroom practically comatose and that was when he saw the open loft hatch. His mother recovered by the morning, by then his idea was coming to fruition and his sanctuary was well on the way. The safe haven made the loud music and drunken rows easier to tolerate. They were, after all, customary of most nights. The place of solace that he created allowed him to escape. He could think and work. The noise remained but the volume was dulled, like his senses.

The blame game continued, as did his headache. Trawling through rotten memories actually made him feel better, it justified his actions and excused the sad, destructive person he had become.

Grammar school had been as far as he got. No one from the rough council estate he lived on went there so it was like starting from scratch but his address meant he was never going to fit in. He only made one friend, Kermit, as he'd been christened, the poor, little runt that got bullied and then one day turned bully. He'd been kinder and called him by his real name, Marty. He could picture those bulging frog eyes even now. Never mind an overactive thyroid, it was his groin that got Marty into trouble.

Marty went one ogle too far when he eyed up Patsie Fisher's tits, which just happened to be the biggest in the fifth year. Marty got off scot-free but he'd got the blame for the leary comment and the resulting whack over the head from her lunchbox. The pain was crippling. He could feel it now. The fact that it was full of cans of cider made it lethal. The box split open, like the skin on his scalp, and the cider and blood spilt, soaking the canteen floor. The trill of the whistle from the supervisor split his brain in two and Mr Daniels, the RE teacher, ran into his fist which resulted in a split lip. Fucking mayhem!

That incident had resulted in his expulsion from school and it destroyed any boyhood dreams he had left. It left a massive mental scar and, ironically, in later years, as his hairline receded, he found a physical scar. An actual dent in his skull. He often wondered if that was the root cause of the migraines as his fingers traced the indentation.

His social circumstances and his mother's reputation ensured his guilt and sealed his fate. Kermit never stuck up for him and Patsie 'Big Tits' Fisher was never going to tell the truth. He vowed there and then, never mind anything else, that he'd never be pussy-whipped.

He had done alright in the end. Faked his CV, upped sticks and moved to London, leaving the shitty memories behind. Miraculously, his marriage and kids had turned out alright. He had climbed the ladder with ease and ended up as a top-of-the-range pencil pusher with a hefty lump sum and pension.

His past, however, had come back to haunt him and the shit really hit the fan big time when the house next door became a holiday let. Tenants were bad enough but this was hell on earth.

He swallowed the prescription painkillers with the dregs from the glass and lay down under the table. He needed to sleep off the migraine if he was to take on that bunch of bolshy bitches next door.

This would, hopefully, be the last weekend. Surely the poor reviews, cursed reputation, and a second unfortunate accident would be the final nail in the coffin...

# CHAPTER 18

I'd once again laid claim to the window seat, my favourite place. Mo was dozing in the armchair, she'd insisted that she was feeling fine just tired. Liz had checked her stitches. They were clean and dry, healing well. I tried to relax but it was impossible, my stomach was churning as I was worried we were about to make a huge mistake.

I let my mind wander and this time I was grateful to be back in the labour ward with Mo as my mentor. She had told me then, and it was certainly true, that I would always remember my first delivery. I was grateful for that special memory and even more so when the vision of my first baby popped into my mind. I languished in that unearthed feeling of complete happiness and unconditional love which never faded. It was so strong it was almost tangible and I could smell the delectable scent of my newborn son's head. It was forever ingrained in my soul. The sweet reminiscence was so real it brought tears to my eyes. I smiled and tried to hold on to it just a little bit longer.

This house definitely evoked strong feelings, whether they were good or bad. My ambivalence about our course of action soon returned and I was unsettled again. I could hear the wind blowing through the hallway, it carried the laughter from the garden. The laughing and joking from the hot tub had got louder. Emma was enjoying forty winks, but not for much longer. She stretched and went to put some music on before making her way outside. I followed her, intending to get drink orders.

For some reason, instead of following the path up to the hot tub, she deviated to the right along the back of the house. I saw something glinting on the floor in the split second before she disappeared. Time seemed to stop and reset itself so that the events before my eyes rolled out in torturous slow motion...

The music continued, as did the laughing and joking in the hot tub. Emma's posture changed, as did her stride. It looked like she was about to reach down for something. There was a modest creak as the rotten wood gave way beneath her feet. The brittle timber splintered upwards with dust and debris as she fell through the hole that was hidden beneath. I winced, expecting a bone-shattering thud, but it was a splash that I heard as she hit the ground. It all happened in a split second.

There was a mad scramble from the tub.

Rachel slipped and twisted her ankle.

Karen lost her bikini top then shrieked as she almost trod on her own breast as she reversed down the steps.

I edged forward, aware that the ground was unstable. I found myself peering into a square, drain-size hole that had opened up and swallowed Emma whole.

I was relieved to see that she was actually still standing, ankle-deep in murky water. She was alternating between laughing and crying but miraculously she appeared uninjured.

'Get me out,' she stammered. Her teeth were chattering with shock and the cold. Her eyes were wild and focused on me. I knew she daren't look around and just as well.

Mo had heard the commotion and had got the torch and rope from the shed. Emma had fallen into some sort of cellar. The stone walls inside matched the rock face. It was like an underground cave. The walls were covered in green slime, cracks indented the back wall and water trickled down. The echo of the dripping water was torturous.

'Oh my God!' cursed Rachel. 'Emma, are you injured?'

'No, but get me out of here,' she said slowly, enunciating each word as her fear increased. I saw a rat swim behind her and hoped no one else would notice, least of all her.

Hoisting her up was relatively easy. Well, a damn sight easier than hauling a woman from a birthing pool in an emergency! By now she was actually laughing with relief and almost high from her near-death experience.

'I have decided that black cats are most definitely unlucky,' said Liz, hissing at the cat on the wall. It spat back and raised its haunches, doubling in size. She stumbled backwards at the sight of its claws, straight into a huge bunch of stinging nettles.

Jill took Emma inside to check she wasn't injured. This was turning out to be a working weekend and we would be lucky to escape with our lives the way things were going. Karen took photos before we replaced the metal drain lid that someone had removed. The hole had been purposely covered with thin, rotten fence panels that would never have taken even a child's weight. It was an accident waiting to happen.

'This place is a death trap,' stated Karen. 'Never mind bad reviews! When Health and Safety hear about this tomorrow, no one will ever set foot in here again.'

My intuition told me that was exactly the plan. And we had fallen for it, hook, line and sinker!

Emma had showered and was resting in the easy chair next to Mo. She was very upbeat considering. 'Not even a bruise,' she boasted.

Rachel had a sock full of ice wrapped around her ankle. 'At least it's all the same leg,' she sighed, rubbing her knee.

Liz was rubbing one of her homemade antihistamine creams on her ass to fight off nettle rash.

'You're quiet, Karen,' said Amy, holding back a laugh.

Karen spluttered her lime and soda down herself and burst out laughing.

'I've got a huge bruise on my boob,' she shrieked. 'It looks just like a hickey!'

'I've never heard of a love bite the size of a foot,' mocked Amy.

'Oh, I have!' Emma gloated.

'I got off lightly compared to you lot,' Emma admitted. 'I noticed my silver watch was missing yesterday and I saw it on the ground, that's why I headed that way. Looks like another setup. I suggest you all check your belongings in case anything else has been taken.'

I offered to go and check upstairs, remembering we were supposed to be watching the loft hatch now we knew it was a potential mode of entry.

'Shut the door for a while,' pleaded Jill. 'That smell is horrendous.'

'Bad enough to put you off supper?' Amy questioned, even though she knew the answer. No matter how bad a day at work or play, it never affected our appetites.

'I'm famished,' whined Emma. 'I'm weak and shaky,' she continued, holding out her trembling hands.

'Well, I'm not surprised. You've had quite a shock. We all have,' said Mo.

The cold hallway was soothing. Its refrigeration effect helped subdue the rotten smell which seeped up through the floorboards. I stopped on the first stair as the air was even colder. It prickled at the nape of my neck and I felt my hair flutter with the icy breeze. I knew there was no wind outside as it was a warm, sticky evening. I turned around to investigate and as my hand touched the bannister I flinched in shock.

The handrail was freezing, just like a block of ice. It was wooden, oak most probably, but it felt like the ice-cold stainless steel of a mortuary door. I chastised myself for such a crazy thought but almost called Amy for her opinion.

I held my hands in front of the letterbox. Its opening was quiet and still. There was definitely no draught or air current coming through from outside. I froze at the bottom of the stairs. I shivered as the freezing air swirled around my body. Ice crystals revolved around me, it seemed, as I stood paralysed in the vortex. My sanity tore itself from the trance that this enigma was inducing and I rushed up the stairs.

Thankfully, the loft hatch was tightly closed. As I peered down the stairs, I was convinced there would be some sort of aura-like mist but there was nothing to show for the earlier supernatural phenomenon. I wondered if I had imagined it. I quickly checked in all of the rooms, paying particular attention whilst in mine to listen for any mysterious creaks and footsteps. I briefly rooted through my belongings to see if anything was missing but as far as I could see, and cared to remember, there wasn't.

Sunday's supper was a time-honoured tradition. We called it 'cold fayre'. It was a feast of all the leftovers and it was our favourite meal of the weekend.

Mo insisted on resuming her usual role of slicing the ham. There were cold sausages leftover from Saturday's breakfast and Rachel was making bubble and squeak patties. I made the salads and dressings whilst Karen used veggies and cheese to make a frittata. She had already made her famous, delectable coleslaw.

'I hope you aren't using mushrooms,' piped up Amy, trying but failing to be funny. She seemed particularly on edge the way she was flitting around the room. Her hyperactivity was always at its height early evening. It was as if her body clock sensed the day was coming to an end so it needed to release all of its energy. She was right, of course, we'd bought too much food. All the better for the auction tomorrow. We'd decided this year that the money raised would go to a women's refuge centre.

Karen brought the bowl of warm Jersey Royals over, ensuring that they were right by her. They had been boiled with fresh parsley and mint and smelt delicious. We knew she would add lashings of butter to her portion, followed swiftly by a second helping. I glanced at the butcher's best ham on the bone and decided that with all that was going on I deserved a treat. Today, I was a flexitarian. Besides, they'd never eat it all and it would be an act of sacrilege if it went to waste.

Incidentally, no one noticed me eating the ham because I hid most of it under the frittata and they were too busy piling their plates high.

'This is delicious,' sighed Emma.

I suggested that Amy and I take a trip to the pub after supper, which was met with a certain amount of animosity. 'We can see if the neighbour's working and if she is we can gauge her reaction when she sees us.'

'Brilliant idea,' agreed Amy. 'We might be able to get a....' She nearly said 'glass of wine' but averted to 'some information' as she caught my eye.

'Well, you had better keep your wits about you and the kitty can stay here!' Karen stated as she glared at Jill for support.

'Have that last bit of butter,' suggested Amy, shoving the dish in Karen's direction.

Surprisingly, Amy and I both finished eating first.

'We don't want pudding,' Amy said, patting her stomach and pulling it in as she stared at Karen. Speak for yourself. I nodded at Liz, who I felt sure had read my mind. I knew she would save us some or some for me at least.

'Hopefully you won't get indigestion,' Karen sniped. 'Unless, of course, you're planning on drinking an acidic drink.'

'Now there's an idea!' Amy replied sarcastically. 'I haven't had a Pernod and lemonade since I was sixteen!'

She only heard someone remark 'underage' when she was halfway out the door.

'Hang on!' I shouted. 'I'm not going out in slippers.'

She waited at the gate, texting with one finger in an overly exaggerated manner.

'Someone's peeping out the window,' she whispered, keeping her back to me.

I turned around sharply without thinking, just in time to see a figure move away from the window next door.

# CHAPTER 19

We walked briskly downhill to the pub hoping to work off our supper.

It was a warm, balmy evening. The sun was on its slow descent, its shimmer on the sea now just a soft pinky-orange. A flock of sparrows swooped down past our ears, their chirping was frenzied as they quarrelled mid-air. The hedgerow provided the battleground as they fought for their roosting spots.

We intended to go to The Shipwreck as a ruse to flush out the barmaid. If she was working, we could gauge her reaction and maybe start up a conversation. Although we were chatting quite happily, I had the strangest feeling that we were being followed. I could almost hear the footsteps. The downward slope made us pick up the pace and I peered over my shoulder several times expecting to see someone but there was no one.

The house was just visible. Its grey, now familiar shape jutted out from the rock face like a stone carving. My knee jerk response was now all too familiar, I shuddered. The wind cooled as it swept across the sea pleasantly drawing up the cold air. As usual, Amy went into overdrive as we rounded the corner and saw the pub. I looked back again expecting to see the shadow of a stalker hiding around the bend, waiting for us to disappear.

'Come on,' Amy urged. 'Don't dawdle on the way in! Save that for the way out. We'll have to have at least one alcoholic drink,' she stated with a smile, 'or it'll look suspicious. We've not walked all the way down here for fruit juice. I bet she doesn't work on a Sunday evening. If it's anything like my local, most staff do the Sunday lunchtime shift. The evening tends to be dead.'

She was spot on, of course. The place was deserted, not a soul in sight, not even behind the bar. We had the place to ourselves so I chose a seat at the back by the window. Its prime location looked over the headland and straight out to sea. The lighthouse was in full view, standing like a pillar of strength, its pose even more striking as the blood-red sun climbed down behind it.

As usual, Amy had gone straight to the bar. She had no patience at the best of times, least of all when she wanted a drink.

'Is this the Marie Celeste?' she called out, then forced a laugh at her own joke.

I scanned the horizon in awe of nature's display which was unfolding before my eyes and I felt sure that the view of the red sun setting behind Lundy Island would be unforgettable. The scene was as impressive as the sun's power, though diminishing by the minute, transforming the landscape into a whole new world. No longer Earth but the fiery planet Venus. The headland was barren. There were no trees but its shape was dramatic, the huge igneous rock boulders stood like a giant dam holding back the mighty ocean. The greens, blues and greys were now gone with the daylight, replaced with stark shades of red against the black silhouettes of the rocks. It depicted a world on fire. The sea was calm as it crept slowly to the shore, like a giant flow of lava.

The ring of chimes startled me as the pub door opened but no one came in, the wind must have blown them. I seemed to be unlucky with chimes. Amy had grown impatient and more persistent, she had noticed an old brass bell which she gave a hefty tug. She nodded at me with confidence and nearly fell off the barstool when the swing doors opened and the scowling face of the landlord appeared before her. She put on her politest voice and sweetest smile.

'Sorry to disturb you but we've just called in for a small one.' She then contradicted herself by asking for two large glasses of dry white wine. I tutted but made no attempt to change the order. As she carried the drinks over, beaming from ear to ear, another smiling face appeared above the swing doors. I only got a snapshot but Karen's description replayed in my head.

Oh my God! He does look like Gino and I think he's the chef!

'Sit down quickly,' I beckoned, tugging her shirt.

'Gosh! I thought I was desperate!' she replied, taking a huge glug of wine.

I could hardly get the words out coherently as I tried to whisper using minimal lip movement.

'It's him!' I stammered. 'The man Karen saw in the woods. Our neighbour!' I took a large gulp and the glass tottered. My exuberance had made me clumsy. 'Not that old man you spoke to, this man was in the kitchen. He must be the chef!'

'Oh my god! He could have put something in our food on Friday,' she said in far too loud a voice. By the sound of it, her imagination was running wild just like mine.

'But, he looks so nice...and he smiled,' I added. We drank the wine far too quickly. The smell of his aftershave lingered. We knew it was him. But why?

'Let's go,' I urged. I felt unsettled and confused and wanted to get back before it was totally dark. Alas, that was not to be. Curiosity, stupidity and the large glasses of wine made us take a detour. It was the church spire that put the idea in her head. Foolishly, in typical schoolgirl fashion, we strode arm in arm towards the graveyard.

'I just want to see the headstone once more. I don't remember his name,' she moaned.

It was dusk. The sun had disappeared but its warmth and the pink sky remained as the day neared its end. It seemed much darker when we reached the graveyard, however, as the church cast a long shadow. The air was much cooler and the birdsong had gone.

I regretted my compliance as we passed through the gate and under an arch into the domain of the dead. My earlier bravado had deserted me. Amy hurried ahead, retracing the path that she hoped would lead to the headstone but it all looked different in the dark and we had come in a different gate.

I glanced up at the bell tower as the bats swept back and forth amongst the gargoyles. Their faces were hideous as they stared down at us with scorn. Reassuringly, the pink-grey sky still glimmered behind a huge sycamore tree. Its red leaves glistened like tinsel as the last drop of sunlight shone through. Amy was getting agitated as there was more than one path and dusk had made us disorientated. I glanced towards the trees behind the old stone wall, their branches merged into the blackness and glow worms and fireflies lit up like eyes.

The sound of the groundsman's heavy boots on the turf made me turn and I saw a tall handsome man move quickly from a gravestone. He mustn't have seen us as by the time we had rushed for his assistance he had gone. The wrought iron gate's hinges squeaked as they swung shut behind him closing us in.

'It's here! Where that man was standing,' she gasped excitedly as she looked down at the familiar stone. 'He was called Anthony.'

'Come on!' I said, pulling her more forcefully than I had intended.

The rabbits scattered as we ran up the path to the gate and I glimpsed the tail end of a badger nosing along the wall. Our haste continued as we hurried arm in arm up the hill. I glanced back into the darkness. There was no one there, just the consoling sight of the sea as it rippled with silver waves.

'He must have finished his shift at the pub and be heading back to the house,' she said breathlessly.

We both sniffed the air. The wind was carrying the scent of his aftershave.

It was almost pitch black by the time we got back, yet Mo was only just drawing the curtains. Next door sat in darkness.

'Have you been looking out the window all evening?' I asked Mo.

'Of course! The sunset was stunning. I've taken some photos. Karen also wanted to see if you were walking normally or staggering,' she laughed.

'Well you must have seen him return,' said Amy. 'He works as a chef at the pub. She wasn't there but he was.'

'No one has come up this hill apart from you two,' said Emma confidently.

'And no one went in next door, that's for definite. I've been watching,' stated Karen curtly.

'How many wines did you have?' she questioned, staring Amy in the eyes.

'We only had one,' I answered truthfully and I knew what was coming next. Karen didn't miss a thing, that's why she was always nominated to check everything before CQC inspections. The others had looked away but I knew they were listening intently whilst they pretended to be otherwise occupied. Rachel was fiddling with the bandage on her knee, her ear angled directly at the unfolding argument. Emma was filing her broken nail, glancing sideways at Mo. I caught some covert nudging as Karen's interrogation continued.

'Small or large glasses?' she asked with a smile that Amy didn't see as she'd turned her back, disgusted by the inquisition.

'Large!' Amy shouted. 'Like the extra-large pudding you've scoffed whilst we've been out gathering information.'

'Truce!' shouted Jill ending the cross-examination and rushing over with the sticky toffee puddings that she had saved for us.

'Well you have been gone a long time, considering you only had one drink,' stated Liz diplomatically.

I recounted our adventure in minute detail and they listened in quiet contemplation. 'Well, I think it is pretty obvious that he was in this house yesterday when we were out. The aftershave has given him away, amongst other things.'

'I think his good looks are all part of his deception,' added Liz.

'Yeah, a wolf in lamb's clothing!' scathed Amy. 'Well, I'm a tiger in a pussy's clothing,' she hissed. 'He's in for one hell of a shock!'

I went upstairs to check my phone hoping there would be a message from Roy. There was. He had deciphered the music and had sent a short audio clip of himself playing the tune on his guitar. My stomach churned as I pressed play. I cut it short. I had only heard the first couple of notes but I knew instantly that it was the sad melody that I had heard on our very first night. I rushed downstairs, heady with mixed emotions.

Despite my excitement, I noticed that the lounge door was ajar. The spider could've made its escape. I closed the door, intending to tell them later. For now, I wanted the audio to take centre stage.

'Guess what!' I said loudly. The party music was blaring so I signalled to Emma to turn it off. 'Roy's played the tune on his guitar,' I hesitated before blurting out. 'It's the song I heard Friday night. Someone else might recognise it as well,' I added, looking around for support.

'Oh, I can't wait!' stuttered Karen. Her voice had gone up a notch and she was visibly flustered. 'I'll dim the lights and try the candles again. This is spooky. I wish we had a ouija board,' she added with a quivering voice.

'Be careful what you wish for,' said Amy sternly. 'Don't mess with things you know nothing about.' She spent so much time with dead bodies I don't think she dared let her mind wander and I didn't blame her. No one answered. There were no smiles and the fruitless acclivity that ensued suggested collective nervous energy. The candles lit first time.

Liz was making us all lime and sodas. I noticed that the last bottle of gin had been opened. We had all agreed yesterday to keep it for next year. They must have had a tipple. Pedantic Karen, a hypocrite too. She was in her element, anyone would think we were having a seance. She had even lit incense sticks.

We all sat around the table like a gaggle of excited schoolgirls as the scented smoke spiralled upwards and intertwined with the gentle glow from the candles. The crystal fruit bowl in the centre of the table reflected its rainbow of colours, changing the contours and features of our faces. Eerie shapes and shadows crept around the room like uninvited guests at a party. The incense smoke twirled and gathered around the centre of the table like an aura. We sipped our drinks and waited in anticipation for the mysterious melody.

The door to the hallway was wedged open so that we could keep tabs on the landing though, admittedly, our surveillance was somewhat haphazard. I was just about to press play on my phone when we heard a loud crash next door. There were raised voices and by the sound of it a full-blown row was in progress. Amy ran to get an empty glass. She placed it against the wall in the hallway and signalled for us to be quiet. The voices were getting louder and the language more colourful. Then suddenly it stopped.

'Someone's sobbing,' Amy whispered. We heard their front door slam. Jill rushed to the window just in time to see the woman rushing to her car in tears.

'There you go!' said Rachel, peering over Jill's shoulder. 'I thought it all along. I don't think she's a willing co-conspirator.'

'Shame she wasn't at the pub earlier,' said Amy. 'We could have slipped her some self-help information.'

'There's not a lot we can do unless she asks for help and we need to be careful we don't make the situation worse and endanger her,' I added. 'Let's hope she stays away tonight.'

'Let's leave the music off now,' Mo suggested. 'It can't be much fun for any neighbours on a Sunday night. After all, we wouldn't normally play music at 11 o'clock at night and we wouldn't normally stay in a semi.'

'Let's listen to the audio clip,' I stammered, hurrying back to the table.

We returned to our seats and the spooky atmosphere returned.

I pressed play.

The gentle acoustic ballad that echoed around the room was hauntingly beautiful. I was also secretly very impressed by Roy's performance. I could tell by the looks on Jill and Liz's faces that they too had heard this tune before. Its intricate melody suggested that whoever had written it had intended for it to be a poignant love song. It was beautiful yet melancholic and I felt sure it depicted the story of lost love. The tune wasn't easily forgotten. It was now etched in my memory forever, especially as Roy had played it.

The audio ended quite abruptly but the wooden flooring and high ceilings made it echo, or so we thought. We had all shut our eyes with the pleasure it induced. As the sad melody continued, however, I soon realised that it wasn't an echo.

I stood up in shock. The candles were flickering violently.

The others were trance-like and oblivious as they thought it was still the audio playing on my phone. My brutal rap on the table was quite out of place. Their startled, confused faces looked directly at me. The colours from the candles dappled their features so they were almost unrecognisable. I knocked on the table again.

'It's not the phone,' I rasped, blowing out a candle with my wrath.

Had I gone crazy, was it just me hearing it? One by one they tiptoed to the hallway, following the music. Lambs to the slaughter.

We all looked up the stairs at the flickering lightbulb.

The loft hatch was tightly closed but the mysterious guitar music echoed inside.

I took the lead and hand in hand we ascended the staircase.

# CHAPTER 20

We were shit scared, but who wouldn't be?! The whole fiasco was surreal. Emma had fled downstairs in tears with Jill close behind her. The rest of us remained on the landing, petrified.

Then the music stopped.

The lightbulb sizzled then shattered which caused a power trip.

We were now in complete darkness.

I could hear Emma whining downstairs and there was a nervous laugh from Jill, which was scary in itself. We huddled together too terrified to move. Amy was gripping me so hard it was painful. She was muttering a prayer of some sort but there was nervous laughter in between so I wondered if she was winding us up. It was Liz that finally plucked up the courage to say something and it was nothing positive.

'There's a lunatic up there, playing that old guitar,' she whispered. 'He's trying to scare us.'

'Well, it's working,' I whispered back.

By now we were all gripping each other. Amy's teeth were chattering loudly and vibrated through us. I was surprised at how scared she was considering that she worked in a mortuary. Slowly but surely we retreated down the stairs like we were chained together. As we reversed into the dining room, my relief was cut short. There on the wall above the lounge door, lit up by a moonbeam, was the huntsman spider in all of its glory. Its long, hairy legs splayed open like some sick centrefold. There was no reaction from the others so I knew they hadn't seen it. Be grateful for small mercies.

'Calm down!' Karen was pleading. 'There has got to be a rational explanation.' I think she genuinely wanted one as she was very pale-faced, aghast.

'Yes!' seethed Liz. 'A psychopathic maniac is in the loft playing the guitar before he murders us.' She sounded near hysterical. Then a familiar noise intruded, though fortunately not Amy's bowels. The car engine was a welcome distraction and I'm sure it averted mass hysteria. Mo tiptoed to the window and peeped out, just in time to see the woman returning.

'Maybe she has been out to get an axe,' joked Amy. Nobody laughed.

'Who has been in the lounge?' I asked, changing the subject but making the matter worse.

'Why?' pleaded Emma, who was still hiding behind a cushion.

'I noticed the door was open earlier. It must've been the wind.' I immediately regretted that I had mentioned it. My indiscretion was a careless slip of the tongue and added to the panic.

'Oh no!' she cried. 'Anything but that spider!'

'Don't be so ridiculous,' scorned Amy. 'We're dealing with a psychopath, never mind an arachnid. Besides, you won't see it in the dark. Pull yourself together!'

Her harsh tone inspired confidence and our camaraderie returned. After three, two, one, we raced to the dining room. Our place of safety.

The house remained in darkness and it was deathly quiet. Not a sound came from next door, nor a creak from the house's old oak skeleton. There was also no wind, which was most bizarre. We sat side by side at the table and went over our plans by candlelight. It was midnight. We were tired and afraid but our bullish arrogance made us determined to see it through. I discreetly checked the hallway and found that the spider was nowhere to be seen, which was not wholly a good thing and added to my increasing anxiety.

Soon it was time for the stakeout.

Jill and Emma slumped together on a bean bag by the front door. They were both clutching their phones as they needed to call the police at the optimal moment. Karen bolted the back door and settled on a chair with her feet up, reading her Kindle. She was quite upbeat and insisted that she was fine on her own. Maybe she was a weird adrenaline junkie? The rest of us were stationed upstairs, just inside our rooms where we could keep watch on the loft hatch.

The night dragged on and it was starting to feel like a tedious nightshift. The quiet ones, which were rare, were often the worst. Boredom combined with tiredness meant that minutes felt like hours. Clock watching was torturous as we were all knackered from the previous night's fiasco. Amy was dozing on her bed whilst I kept watch at the bedroom door. I lay on the floor propped up on pillows. It was much the same arrangement in the other rooms. It would be a miracle if we managed to stay awake.

The gentle hooting of an owl in the distance coaxed me to close my weary eyes.

I must have fallen asleep, momentarily I hoped. I could hear snoring so I knew I wasn't alone. The house was silent. I looked at my watch and was surprised to see that it was 2 o'clock in the morning.

It was very subtle but instantly recognisable.

The sweet smell of aftershave.

My heart began thumping in my chest, my throat dry. The lump that formed made it impossible to swallow let alone speak. I felt paralysed. It took all my strength and willpower just to tilt my head so I could see outside the bedroom door.

Was I ill with a fever? My skin was hot and feverish yet I felt cold and shivery. Surely I must be febrile and hallucinating?

The landing was dark but a hint of moonlight beamed across the stairs. I watched and listened in fascination as the hypnotism began. By now, I was a willing participant. It was euphoric. The moonlight changed shape before my eyes. It must have been the clouds passing by outside.

A silver and white shape danced in circles at the top of the stairs. It was transparent, like a silk spider web forming its mass. I looked for the spider hoping it would explain this strange wonder. Meanwhile, the draught of cold air brewing downstairs began advancing upwards. By the time it reached the landing, its whistle was a low, feral howl and its coldness an arctic blast. I remained bewitched. An indescribable presence soothed me.

The smell of cologne was stronger than ever and the wind banged the doors which roused the others. I was unsure if they could see what had appeared before me as no one uttered a sound. I was in complete awe of my surroundings whilst they waited with bated breath and trepidation, blissfully unaware of the vision that seduced me.

Our senses were heightened with expectation and we all heard it the instant that the wind suddenly disappeared. First a brash scraping noise followed by muffled creaks and then the distinctive sound of soft footsteps.

The signal was given just as the loft began to open...

I snapped out of my trance, adrenaline surged and I realised that there was no going back. In a mad panic I fumbled for the torch but I couldn't find it. We all waited, eager to pounce, every muscle fibre and sinew tense and taut. I willed for it to be over. I willed for us to be safe.

The ladder eased down in silence, its workings had obviously been oiled in advance. Then the shadow began its descent, which seemed to be in slow motion. That gave our terror time to heighten.

Our eyes had adjusted to the dark allowing us to take stock of the intruder. Whoever it was was dressed all in black.

Halfway down the ladder, the head turned towards us. At that very minute, the moonlight shone in like a spotlight to reveal two menacing red eyes inside a black balaclava. A scream almost pierced my eardrum.

My eyes diverted back to the circles of moonlight which were now swirling like Saturn's rings at the top of the stairs. There was an almighty surge of freezing air that swept the illumination into the lightbulb, which then crackled like a sparkler before swinging violently back and forth. It produced a flickering light so bright that it dazzled the impostor but gave us the pathway and courage we needed.

Before we had even moved, he was falling. He gripped the rickety ladder with one hand as he slipped and lost grip of the box in the other. It split apart and a huge rat burst forth, taking a chunk of his thumb before making a hasty escape.

Amy sprang like a wild cat, grabbing his joggers from behind.

He was short and stocky, full back material, so he easily stood his ground. She had landed on the floor but had pulled his jogging bottoms down with her and was hanging on for dear life. I stood over her for protection as he thrashed around swearing whilst trying to free his legs.

'You crazy fucking bitch!' he spat.

The look on Liz's face was vicious as she psyched herself up. The twisted pillowcase with the bar of soap inside was a lethal weapon and it was becoming more powerful with each hefty swing. As he managed to free one leg and step forward, she took aim and swung it like a hockey stick and, bullseye, whacked him with brutal force straight in the bollocks.

The yelp was blood-curdling. His hands instinctively went to his groin and he fell flat on his face. He was covered in blood from his thumb and so was much of the landing, everything felt wet and tacky.

Karen had shot up the stairs. He was squealing like a pig as she pulled off the mask. She let out a gasp and staggered back in surprise.

'It's not him!' Her voice was joyous, in stark contrast to Rachel who was pent up ready for a rugby tackle.

Mo sauntered over. 'You piece of shit! You could have killed me! You sick bastard!'

We had never heard her swear before.

The whole escapade was over in minutes. The bang on the front door was frenzied and brought us back to our senses. It was the police, which was strange as Jill was still giving details on the phone. Emma opened the door and they stampeded up the stairs.

The woman next door was standing outside in tears.

She must have made the call.

# CHAPTER 21

It was pandemonium as another police car had arrived for backup. They soon realised that was surplus to requirements as the perpetrator had been cautioned, arrested and cuffed in minutes. To say he was shell-shocked was an understatement. The arresting officer led him out to the other police car to be taken into custody. Liz had been civil enough to check his thumb wound. Though initially it had bled profusely, it was actually just superficial. A tiny nick. It had stopped bleeding so she had given him a plaster.

'Hope you're up to date with your tetanus,' she spat as they led him out the door.

He was walking like he'd spent the day on a carthorse. His hunched posture suggested his ego had been severely dented, but I'm pretty sure that paled in comparison to the pain from the ball bashing. The officers were professional but we couldn't miss the smirks and the stifled laughter as they liaised with the other squad car.

'Would you like a cushion?' We heard an officer say with feigned empathy.

Oddly, the power to the house had returned of its own accord so Karen proceeded to make everyone a coffee. The officers did a quick scout of the house to make sure we were safe and that there were no other unwanted visitors. We had already assured them that we had not sustained any physical injuries. They took a brief history of what had happened but it soon became apparent that this wasn't a straightforward break-in.

We omitted the fact that we had actually suspected this might happen and that we had lain in wait, as we knew in all honesty that our actions were foolish and we should have involved the police beforehand. Luckily, no one had been seriously injured. They told us that they were confident that we had acted in self-defence and within the law, so we had nothing to worry about.

Our account of events prompted more than a few raised eyebrows. The grand finale made for awkward listening for the police officers, provoking a sharp intake of breath from Pete and a wince followed by some seat-shuffling from Dermot.

Conscious of the time and our yawns, they were eager to wrap it up as quickly as possible. Pete informed us that a detective would be allocated to the case first thing in the morning. I could swear his voice was an octave higher when he said certain words.

We were also told that a named detective would be assigned as soon as possible and a crime scene investigator would also come to the house to collect evidence. Detailed statements would also be required so we arranged to go to the main police station in the morning before we went home. They decided this was a complex case and advised us that an experienced investigator would most certainly be involved.

I was keen to check out the theory that our food had been tampered with so I broached the subject.

'Mo's blood sample at the hospital was normal. It didn't reveal anything suspicious but it was just a routine test so they only checked for certain things. If our suspicions are correct and we have been drugged, it might still show up in a urine test,' I said. We had already given them the rundown on the magic mushrooms. Amy had practically shoved the suspect mushroom in Dermot's face.

'You can provide urine samples at the station tomorrow,' Pete advised.

'Magic mushrooms! I've not heard of them in a long time,' Dermot mumbled as he loosened his trousers from around his groin area.

'A rotting animal carcass under the floorboards you say?' asked Pete as they passed through the hallway. I could see his nostrils flaring before he held his breath.

'The forensics guy will delve into that tomorrow. I suggest you all get some rest and be careful. Stay inside! That open drain could have had fatal consequences.'

Judging by the looks on their faces, they were dubious about the whole thing. They headed next door, presumably to question the woman.

We couldn't wait to get to our beds. I was the last to go up, for some reason I was lingering. I went to check that the back door was bolted. I noticed that the door of the small pantry, used to store the hoover and cleaning essentials, was ajar. I peered inside and there was the huge rat, lying flat on its back with its legs in the air. I gulped in astonishment before prodding it with my foot. It was definitely dead, as Amy would say. Perhaps one of the police officers had killed it.

The answer came shortly. In the hallway, curled up in a ball, just below the front door was a black cat. Most likely the tomcat that we kept seeing in the garden. He was in a good mood judging by his purring and I was grateful for his intervention so I left him to sleep. A subtle ray of early sunlight shone through the window. Its beam warmed the hallway and I welcomed the contrast, as did the cat. The rose gold light glimmered on its shiny, black fur, the warmth had more than likely induced its catnap. If we were lucky, it might get the spider. In all honesty, I liked spiders. They were fascinating and secretly I thought it was a shame that the rat had not escaped.

I trudged wearily up the stairs to a symphony of snoring. I looked away from the bathroom, ignoring the eight black legs that protruded from behind the sink. I was knackered.

It was just before daybreak as I lay in bed. The house was strangely calm. I could hear the sea in the distance, the waves gently lapping to the shore. I suddenly found myself sitting on a beach with my mother, tucked in between her legs with my head against her heartbeat. She had her arms tightly around me and I could feel the sand between my toes as we watched my father swimming out to sea. Her warmth and love embraced me as I breathed in her scent. I felt safe in deep nostalgic sleep and I welcomed the feeling.

Unsurprisingly, we all overslept the next morning. Amy's phone bleeped with a text message. If it wasn't for that, God knows what time we would have awoken.

The last morning would typically involve a lot of tedious cleaning but, thankfully, we had been given strict instructions not to do that. We could pack our belongings but everything else was to be left as it was.

When I got downstairs, I wasn't surprised to find that the cat had gone. The dead rat was still in the cupboard so I left it there.

'That black cat that we kept seeing slept in the hallway last night. I think it killed the rat,' I stated. No one answered, they were all too busy packing and judging by their troubled features they were probably churning over last night's dramatic events.

The smell in the hallway was rank but we all commented on how warm it now felt. That would worsen the smell, for sure, so it was just as well we were leaving.

What a welcome for the investigation team. Although, I was pretty sure that they were used to a lot worse.

It was another glorious sunny day that spurred us on. We had coffee and biscuits on the go whilst packing, having decided that we would treat ourselves to a full English breakfast at our favourite café. It was a family-run affair and had an unrivalled beachside position. It was located in the picturesque seaside town en route to the police station, which fitted in with our arrangements. That way we would be set up for the tedious time at the police station and the onward journey home. Hopefully, we wouldn't need any lunch!

We also had something else to look forward to...

There was a definite buzz in the air and excitement was building as all the leftover items were placed in the centre of the table for the annual auction.

We all grabbed our reusable carriers ready to bag our wares. Year-on-year it was always the same scenario. The mumbles about not really wanting anything whilst discreetly eyeing something you really, really wanted. There was always cheating. I had already sneaked two limes and a beer for Roy.

We knew Amy would be planning her evening meal and she would go to extraordinary lengths to ensure she got the right ingredients. Karen would be bound to question her, as always, proclaiming what a strange recipe she was concocting. 'Why has it always got to be served with baked beans?' was usually the first question and it would inevitably build up to an argument.

In Karen's eyes, she should have the first choice of anything vegetarian. Amy knew that only too well, so she would always bid for the beans or tomatoes. I noticed there was a tin of baked beans already in Amy's bag, along with half a bottle of white wine.

We mulled around seemingly not caring but all eyes were on Karen and she knew it. Monday morning guaranteed that she would be the centre of attention. She would go to the head of the table with a wooden spoon when she was ready and not before.

There was a gasp as she began banging the table to signal the start.

It was followed by an almighty scream from Emma. The spider had crawled out from the bag of tangerines and was in the middle of the table.

Amy moved swiftly and just about managed to trap it under an extra-large lunch box.

The others had scarpered.

The spider was playing dead. Its long legs had vanished as it had coiled into a tight black ball. This was to her advantage as she managed to put the lid on the box and then ran into the garden holding it at arm's length. We didn't think about what she was doing. We both just wanted to set it free. She pulled off the lid and flung the box into the air in a haphazard manner. It looked like a miniature parachute as it floated to freedom. Its hairy legs provided just enough resistance and the wind whisked it far away.

'You should have kept it as evidence,' Karen hollered from the bedroom window.


Karen, like us, was anxious to proceed with the auction as time was ticking by.

'Pull yourselves together,' she said, glaring at Emma. 'The spider's gone, thanks to Amy.' Her tone was as if Amy had done us a disservice and it provoked a reaction. The long, drawn-out intake of breath from Amy seemed to blow her up, making her at least a foot taller.

'Oh, here we go again,' sighed Mo.

The others looked really pissed off.

But before Amy had the chance to retaliate, or even breathe out, Karen had placed an expensive bottle of pinot grigio in front of her as a reward. She must have saved it especially. I wondered if it would cause a fight. It would have last year. There were smiles. Amy had obviously come to terms with the fact that it was now her favourite tipple.

The auction proceeded swiftly and, as usual, we all ended up with what we wanted. The money it raised would be added to the money left over in the kitty. As always, we had a decent amount for our chosen charity.

Our bags were packed and we were just about to leave when there was a knock at the door.

# CHAPTER 22

'You'd better come in,' we heard Rachel saying in a soft, sympathetic voice.

'It's the woman from next door,' whispered Amy as she skittered around us like a meerkat on speed.

'I just wanted to explain a few things,' she said, as Rachel brought her through to the kitchen. 'I'm Sue, by the way.'

Her manner was composed with a hint of embarrassment or maybe she was just feeling shy. It must have taken a lot of courage, in more ways than one, for her to approach us.

In our line of work, we were used to responding appropriately in awkward situations and we were skilled at communicating with people from all walks of life. After all, a labouring woman was probably at her most vulnerable and we dealt with that at work daily. Gaining a woman's trust was half the battle and I was sure that would be needed in this situation.

Rachel honed in on Sue's almost tangible fragility. Her experience and calming manner soon put her at ease.

'I'll make some coffee,' offered Amy, 'or tea if you'd like?'

'Now there's a surprise!' interjected Karen, this time trying to lighten the mood and not Amy's temper.

We didn't all sit down initially as we figured it would be quite intimidating, one of her and eight of us.

Her voice was meek as she tiptoed from her shell, testing the water. We all made small talk about the house and its stunning views and she kept repeating how envious of our friendship she was and that she missed her friends and family. She started to open up and just as well as I could tell Amy was getting impatient.

'I'm going to the police station later to give a full statement but I felt I owed it to you to provide some sort of explanation for ruining your weekend.'

'It has been quite an adventure,' said Liz. 'We have definitely not been bored!'

'Well, it all got out of hand,' Sue continued. Her voice was shaky now and when she glanced at Mo's head wound she began visibly trembling.

'I survived a fall down a drain,' joked Emma. 'I was more upset when I broke a nail slapping my own ass.'

We were all sitting down by now, the ice was broken and she was ready to tell us what she wanted to...

She began by explaining that their retirement dream had turned into a nightmare. The owner of the house we were staying in had moved back to London and let the house out. Unfortunately, noisy tenants had stirred up lots of unresolved issues in her husband's past. Not only that, he had found it difficult adjusting to the new way of life that comes with retirement. Moving house and to a new area all at the same time had been a serious error of judgement.

He had suffered from depression in the past but this time it was much worse and he had refused to seek help. He was adamant that it was the noise causing the problem.

She broke eye contact and struggled to form the next sentence.

'The final tenant, the guitarist, who had the unfortunate accident, was the beginning of a dark, slippery slope. I liked hearing him practise but Darren didn't. It drove him insane, literally,' she added, stifling a cry.

Rachel made some reassuring noises which coaxed her to continue. She sipped her coffee, its bitterness showed on her face. She requested sugar. I hoped Amy hadn't thrown it down the sink.

Hopefully that would settle her nerves.

She skirted around the accident, quite obviously not keen to go into details this time. Amy and I exchanged glances and I could see that Amy was annoyed.

'Things improved for a while as the house was empty for a good six months whilst police investigations took place but then out of the blue the owner phoned us to say it was going to be a holiday let. That tipped Darren totally over the edge. It started almost like a game and he seemed to be enjoying it. I knew he was bored so I turned a blind eye initially but as the parties got rowdier so did he. There was no funny side to any of it anymore. He was struck with crippling migraines almost daily brought on by stress. He complained to the owner about the constant flow of noisy guests. Hen and stag parties, large families gatherings, they were all as bad as each other. The complaints got him nowhere so he decided to take matters into his own hands. I imagine that he figured if they complained about their stay and gave bad reviews the bookings might dry up. Chance would have been a fine thing!'

We were all listening intently, the reference to reviews had caused Karen to almost choke on her coffee.

Sue continued. She was in full flow now as the memories came flooding back.

'It was just minor things to begin with, pranks almost. Like throwing woodlice in through the open windows and sugar to attract ants. The day guests were due to arrive he would put rubbish and cat shit in the garden. But it was all to no avail. The guests kept coming and the

177

noise got louder. I wish that I had been able to help him before it all went too far but he shut me out.'

She finished her coffee and then continued.

'He was spending more and more time in our loft conversion, it was quieter there. Besides, the migraines were incapacitating. The loft was his so-called safe haven so I rarely went up there. The last time I did I was shocked. I knew that he had been ordering and collecting things but I didn't realise the magnitude of it all. After I spotted a huge black spider in a tank, that was it, never again.' She shuddered, as did Emma.

'I was totally out of my depth. I knew if I confronted him...,' she looked down and then changed tack. 'Actually, in all honesty, I think I was naive and stupid. I didn't know what he was up to or what he was capable of,' she stammered, chewing her bottom lip until it bled.

We had all noticed the fresh bruises on her upper arms and she knew we had. She stifled a cry and Jill rushed for a box of tissues.

'We had a row Saturday night. I had plucked up the courage to look in the loft as I was worried about his state of mind and about what he was planning. That's when I saw the doorway through. He must've made that when the house was empty. I'm sure it wasn't there before the accident. Anyway, I won't ramble on too much and bore you.'

'Oh, we're definitely not bored,' several of us said together.

I noticed Amy had her elbows on the table with her chin in her hands. I nudged her and immediately regretted it as she asked in a callous tone, 'Why did you tell us, in gory detail, about the accident when we were in the pub on Friday night? That put a dampener on our weekend straight away.'

Her answer was spontaneous and fluent.

'He was getting desperate. The house had been given a few bad reviews but its prime location still attracted people. It was booked every weekend, there was no respite. He was deluded by then, I'm sure. I think it was a last-ditch attempt to end the misery. I guess he thought that no one likes a house with a bad history. He banked on you going to the pub on the first night as the other guests did.'

She paused and took stock of herself, surely debating whether or not to utter another word. She found the will and courage to continue but was unable to control her emotions.

'I was to tell you about Anthony dying,' she began, sobbing as she said his name, 'and I was supposed to put these in your drinks.' She produced a small, clear pot containing eight white pills. 'I'm taking them to the police station for analysis.'

Amy was shocked into silence, as we all were.

My chair scraped the floor but the wincing was not from touching a raw nerve but from the disclosure. I stood up as I had something important to say.

'Sue, do you think there's a possibility that Anthony's death was not accidental?'

They all looked at me, then directly at Sue. I heard the word 'murder' bounce around the room in hushed tones. Sue must have heard it too.

She took her time mulling it over. When she answered it was with confidence and finality. 'To be totally honest, that did cross my mind a while back, but no, Darren was with me, and besides, at that point, I'm pretty sure that he had no means of entering the house. Anyhow, he wouldn't do that. He's not capable of...'

Her voice was now a mere murmur so we didn't hear her final words.

'Well, he frightened Mo half to death,' said Rachel. 'She saw him at the top of the stairs Saturday evening. That's what made her collapse.'

'No! That's impossible,' she stated clearly and sternly. 'We were together at the pub all evening. We got back late. In fact, we had just got in the door when we saw the ambulance arrive. I admit he was delighted, said you were all pissed. If he did anything, it definitely wasn't in the evening.'

We all looked at Mo who had turned a deathly shade of pale. 'But I smelt his aftershave,' she droned in a monotone voice.

'Darren never wears aftershave. You must be mistaken.' Her eyes glazed over momentarily as if she was remembering something poignant.

'I suppose he doesn't play the guitar either?' asked Jill.

'No, certainly not, as I said before he hates music of any kind.'

Karen downed a glass of cold water as if she was trying to flush the bitterness from her voice before she spoke. She was calm and collected when she began and stared Sue directly in the eyes.

'I saw you yesterday, early afternoon. You were arguing with another man. The chef from the pub, I believe.' Karen paused as if she was reliving the memory. She made a sound like a gruff tut and her tone this time echoed of distrust and jealousy. 'You were on that little common not far from here.'

Yet again Sue's answer came quickly. I looked at her eyes to see if they strayed to the left. I'd read that they do if you lie.

'Oh yes, that was Marco. You are right. He's a chef and we work together at the pub. We've become friends...recently friendlier. He wanted me to meet him that evening but I said no. I've been trying to break it to him gently that I don't want a relationship. I admit he makes me happy, and, if I'm honest, I was enjoying the attention and the compliments.'

'And the kiss?' Karen interjected, sounding like a frustrated, cross-examining barrister.

'It was just a kiss,' she replied with conviction. Her inner spirit seemed to re-emerge from a deep, hidden place and her posture reflected it. She was now sat bolt upright oozing confidence and her eyes shone with tears and honesty.

What's in a kiss? I could certainly empathise. I got up to get myself a glass of water and I could feel the eyes on my back. The cold water stifled my blush. Hopefully, it would disappear before I turned around. I need not have worried as all eyes were on Sue as I walked back to the table. I had a distinct feeling that she was deliberating her next move.

'I'll be honest with you,' she said. Her eyes were definitely brimming with tears which she just about held back. 'It was Tony I was in love with but we didn't stand a chance. It was all taken away that terrible night.'

She gasped with passion and despair which seemed to resonate around the room. A ray of sunlight, so bright that we had to shield our eyes, shone directly on her face exposing her sorrow. I felt sure that the feelings that she had laid bare before us were genuine. It was all very dramatic, to say the least, and it was set to continue.

Amy stood up as if she was possessed by the sunlight or just plainly possessed. She gathered the mangled music sheets together and handed them to Sue.

'I couldn't make out the title,' she said with uncharacteristic emotion. 'But now it's crystal clear. It says Sue.'

Sue held the song tightly, still fighting back the tears. 'I need to go,' she said abruptly, 'but thank you for everything.'

'Your cat slept in the hallway last night,' I called out.

'We haven't got a cat,' she answered. 'Darren hates them. There was a black one hanging about weeks ago, kept digging up our garden before it disappeared.'

Rachel pushed past us. She was anxious to give her some helpline numbers and information. They also exchanged phone numbers before Rachel came back inside, letting out a long sigh as she slumped in the chair.

'This is all a bit surreal,' she said in dismay.

'You can say that again,' Mo replied as she too plonked herself down.

Under normal circumstances, we would have all sat round to hammer it out but there was nothing normal about this weekend. Besides, we didn't have the time as we had an agenda to meet and we were soon to be reminded.

'Chop-chop!' snapped Karen, bringing us back to some sort of normality.

'We can discuss it over BREAKFAST,' she emphasised, knowing that food was one of the main driving forces behind us all.

She was spot on as Emma was already heaving bags out the door.

I offered to do a quick scout of the house to check that we had not forgotten anything. That scenario had not yet occurred in all of the years we had gone away.

I went up the stairs one last time. It was uncanny the way the cold had disappeared yet there was still quite a breeze blowing outside, enough to make the letterbox rattle. I noticed the Tamarix tree bending like a contortionist.

Be grateful, I told myself. The strange, intense atmosphere had gone. The old house seemed at peace. Indeed, it was peaceful but it felt like something was missing. Dare I say personality? Now, where would we be without that?

I quickly checked in all of the rooms and glanced at the loft hatch again. As I descended the stairs, I knew the house had changed. I couldn't feel anything anymore. It was just bricks and mortar.

'Hurry up!' shouted Liz from the car. 'We've got a busy day ahead!'

I looked behind as we drove away and smiled. They had all seen it as well. Laughter filled the air just like when we had arrived.

The last part of the house sign had blown away.

'Goodbye, Windy Ass!' laughed Amy.

'Well I hope so!' said Karen smirking. 'That really would be a godsend.'

# CHAPTER 23

The crisp sea breeze blew in through the car's windows. Hopefully, its coolness would keep us awake, as I noticed that we all kept yawning intermittently. Undoubtedly because we had only had a few hours sleep. I relished the fresh, salty sea smell which was a heavenly change from the awful odour that we had reluctantly grown accustomed to at the house. My attention was drawn to the road as we passed a crime scene investigation van speeding around the bend, undoubtedly heading up the hill to Windy Passage.

'Plenty of Monday morning gossip for the locals this week,' remarked Mo.

'I presume that the police have got keys?'

'Of course, they have,' said Karen. 'And the owner's been informed. Apparently, he's meeting them there. It's strange and highly suspicious, considering the fact that this is the second time there's been a police investigation on his property. I'm sure, like myself, the police don't believe in coincidences.'

To Karen's annoyance, Liz was leading in the other car. She had managed to get ahead as Karen had waited for me to lock up the house. However, in no time at all both cars were cruising into the seafront car park. As soon as the opportunity arose, Karen raced past Liz and hastily parked, almost scraping the posh car on her near side. Some things never change and I was grateful for the normality as this weekend had been quite the contrary.

Our destination was a small, seasonal tourist town that turned into a ghost town in the winter. It had been built up alongside a renowned surfing beach that influenced the whole look of the place. The surf school and the hire shop domineered the seafront along with the one hotel.

Most of the shops sold beachwear and everything a surfer dude could ever want. Mo was quick to notice a sale sign, which acted as a magnet as she veered in its direction. There were no charity shops here but a sale was second best as far as she was concerned. Liz and Rachel were about to follow her.

'We've no time for shopping,' Karen insisted cantankerously.

There was a delicious smell in the air and that soon diverted their interest. Nothing took precedence over food. Karen was already marching towards our favourite café with Amy hot on her heels sniffing the bacon like a bloodhound. They raced past a couple foolish enough to be lingering outside. Karen rushed in ahead of Amy and the reason for the couple's dithering became apparent.

'It's full!' she sniped, glaring at her watch like it was to blame.

'We need to come back in half an hour. Damn tourists!'

Amy had barged in after, hoping to be told something different I suppose as she never did like taking no for an answer.

'I've reserved our favourite table by the window,' she informed us a few minutes later when she reappeared.

We split into two groups. Mo escorted the shoppers whilst the rest of us fancied a stroll along the beach. Karen wanted a race, as usual, which was fine as Amy was in our group.

It was a beautiful morning. The few white, cotton wool clouds dotting the blue sky were whisked on their way by the stiff, south-westerly wind blowing off the Atlantic. It was a perfect day for surfing and I knew that Karen would notice. She had stopped mid-stride at the surfing shack where the lifeguards hung out. It was unlike her to halt when she was working up rhythm and speed, so she must have had a good reason and that was exactly what we were worried about.

'Oh no! She's looking at the hire prices,' whispered Rachel.

'Or pretending to!' I added, noticing a muscle-bound lad about her son's age pulling on his wetsuit.

'Goes on easy if you've got muscles,' remarked Amy sarcastically. 'It's fat that puckers up and causes the problem,' she lectured, yanking Karen's arm.

We didn't hear the reply, they were too far ahead by then.

'What a weekend!' said Rachel with a sigh as we strolled along enjoying the view whilst our minds churned things over. There would be no chance of the clean sea air clearing our minds. The whole weekend had been overwhelming, like the waves rising in the distance.

We sat in silence on the sand. The odd squawk of a gull broke up the almighty roar of the powerful rollers that rose before us like turquoise tunnels. Their white tips poised to unfurl and smash their frothy foam on the shore, pounding the sand into fine gold dust.

We decided to walk down to the sea, maybe to paddle, but as we neared the waves their magnitude grew stronger and we knew it was too rough. We could soon feel the spray as it showered our faces, the salt reached our tongues and parched our lips.

Karen and Amy looked small and insignificant in the distance. The wind took our breaths away and the surf drowned out our voices. It was all the more inspiring as the beach was almost empty. We were tiny inconspicuous specks in the sand as we stood on the ocean's boundary. I knew deep inside that boundaries had been broken this weekend. I had seen and felt too much that I couldn't explain. Like the freezing draught, the power surges, and the shape-changing mist. It was the presence that had vanished so suddenly that bothered me the most. I glanced at Rachel who was deep in thought, staring out to sea, and I wondered if it was just me or if we all felt the same.

Amy had stopped and was bent over double, staring at her feet. The tide was on the turn and, for an awful moment, I thought that she had stood on a weever fish as I knew they lurked at low tide. The razor-sharp spikes on the fish's back are laden with poison ready to pierce the skin like a surgeon's scalpel. I remembered the excruciating pain from experience. My mind drifted further and I wondered if Tony had suffered when the shard of glass pierced his neck but, more so, I wondered how it had really happened.

We caught up with Amy and discovered the source of her intrigue. A huge jellyfish, the size of a bicycle wheel.

'It's definitely dead,' she mumbled as she warily poked it with her toe. It was like looking at a creature from another universe. Its clear, gelatinous mass laid bare on the sand. You could see straight through its core which was entwined with shining tunnels and tubes, some of them fluorescent pink. This life form was alien to us, cast out from the sea to die on the barren sand.

'Don't touch it,' Amy cautioned Rachel, who was now bending down with her glasses on. 'We've had a bad experience with jellyfish in the past,' she began, smiling at me.

'I'm all ears,' said Rachel, desperate for distraction from more troubling thoughts.

We sat down on the sand and Amy spun her tale...

'That weekend we went to Spain, Karen took us to a lovely beach near her apartment.'

'The beach with the fishermen?' asked Rachel, winking at me and rubbing her wedding ring up and down.

'No! This beach was further along towards the town. We sunbathed for a while but it was sweltering. Far too hot to lie in the sun as it was mid-July. The beach was crowded as it was the weekend.'

'Karen,' Amy said her name with disdain, 'led us into the water to cool off but she should have known better! It was blissful, so refreshing and relaxing until Mo pointed out how strange it was that no one else was actually in the sea. Karen was oblivious, as usual, swimming up and down showing off her crawl.'

Amy paused to draw breath and at the same time, after checking that Karen was out of earshot, impersonated Karen's breathing by rapidly turning her head from side to side puffing in and out in an overly exaggerated manner.

'Do the arms,' urged Rachel, winding her up and laying the bait. Amy was too tired for a fight today so she handed it over to me.

'Julia!' she nodded to me to continue. So I did...

'I had noticed a big flag flying above the lifeguard's beach tower so I signalled to Karen as we felt sure she would know what the flag meant. She lifted her goggles as a token gesture and flippantly assured us it was nothing to worry about. As long as it wasn't a red flag, we would be fine. Well, Amy was having none of it. I think she sensed a chance to prove Karen wrong. And that, in her eyes, was a goal worth pursuing. We watched as she marched up the beach, dripping all over the sunbathers as she weaved in and out. Quite a few people were laughing, not at her but at us in the water. To her annoyance, sign language wasn't required as he spoke fluent English. We lifted our sunglasses and watched in awe as the lifeguard climbed the watchtower like Poseidon emerging from the sea. He looked in our direction and stretched out the billowing flag to reveal a huge print of a black jellyfish! Karen's front crawl turned gala-speed as she raced to the shore. It was me that got caught mid-breaststroke. The sting across my stomach made me flinch but it was mild, like stinging nettles. Nothing like the pain of standing on a weever fish.'

The cool wind blowing off the waves soon brought us back to the present. Karen had been paddling in the sea. It was never too rough for her.

'What are you going on about?' she asked, as she marched back to join us. She had obviously seen Amy's impersonations.

'Spanish jellyfish!' we laughed. And then she told Rachel her version of events as we walked back to the shore.

The sea air certainly makes you hungry. I was famished.

'I'm starving,' whinged Amy as if she had read my thoughts.

'Well, that's a first for you,' replied Rachel.

This weekend was certainly full of surprises as Amy never used the word starving; it was forbidden by her church cronies.

There was no sign of the others and we weren't surprised as we noticed that virtually all the shops had sale signs in the windows. We sat on some flat rocks to conserve energy. We were in full view so they would be sure to see us. Amy had checked in the café, our table was still occupied and hunger had turned her tongue vicious.

'Greedy holidaymakers by the looks of it,' she cussed. 'They've got mega breakfasts with extra fried bread to mop up the fat,' she rambled to herself. 'People wonder why they get high blood pressure and cholesterol,' she cursed, shaking her head. She had made a point of emphasising the word cholesterol and had glared directly at Karen when she said it.

Karen ignored her remarks, she had her back to us and was unusually quiet and pensive. I felt sure that she must be raking over the events of the weekend.

'I've been thinking about that guitar music. I can't get the tune out of my head,' said Rachel quietly. 'There's got to be a rational explanation.'

'The police will be there by now,' I replied, looking at my watch. 'I am hopeful that they will get to the bottom of it.' I spoke with more confidence than I felt.

We were surrounded by rock pools, freshly filled by the early morning tide, each one a mini-ecosystem teeming with life and fascinating to watch. The natural world was another love of my life and I relished the moment. I knew I was unaware of most of the organisms that existed in the deep, rocky puddle before me, especially the creatures that are invisible to the naked eye. So why would I be aware of every existence? Not everything was visible to the naked human eye. My mind churned over as I explored possibilities that I would have never entertained before this weekend.

Bladderwrack draped the edges of the pool, allowing the shore crabs to creep along camouflaged. I could see a pincer edging its way out, Amy had seen it too.

'Fancy me catching that spider,' she gloated with pride as she attempted to ease out the crab. Alas, it escaped and made a hasty retreat to the bottom of the pool.

The water was crystal clear. We sat in silence observing the sea life, grateful for the opportunity to forget, for a minute, the enormity of what had happened. I fished out a plastic bottle top, worried that a hermit crab might move in. Shrimps danced back and forth, their feelers probing for food. The pool was a hive of activity. It became the ocean's jewellery box as the sunlight streamed through the water, enhancing all of the colours. Limpets and barnacles lined the outside. Red sea anemones sat like rubies just above the surface, their counterparts underwater displaying frilly tentacles like streamers to entice their prey.

That's what we had done this weekend. Set a trap. It was entrapment and I was sure it was illegal and, worse still, it could jeopardise a conviction. I was startled by Karen's voice which drowned out the seagulls.

'It's free,' she shouted, waving us over. She signalled at me to stay put whilst she went to find the shoppers.

'Just in case I miss them!' she hollered.

Amy had rushed in to grab the table. She was soon scanning the menu and admiring the stunning view. She waved at me and beckoned me to join her.

I waited on the rocks as I had been told. The stark instruction had made me nostalgic for childhood caravan holidays. However, I rarely did as I was told as a child. The expanse of grey rocks covered in limpets and mussels reminded me of a childhood family holiday years ago. I had spent virtually the whole day with my sisters and cousins collecting cockles and winkles for the adults. We had ended up with bucket loads of them. I remembered with distaste the smell as they boiled in salted water on the caravan stove. My aunt had spent the entire evening pricking them out with a pin. I could see her now as she sat on the step with the setting sun in the distance.

It was bacon I could smell now and my mouth was watering as the smell wafted seaward from the café. Karen had soon rounded them up. I was surprised she had to as they were bound to be hungry as it was nearing midday. We were chuffed with our table. It was definitely the best in the café and well worth waiting for. We all had a sea view but at the moment the menu took centre stage.

We placed our orders promptly, the sea air had notched our hunger up to an all-time great. I decided on the spur of the moment to be veggie today. As usual, nature watching had made me feel guilty. Karen and I ordered the large veggie option, the others had the mega classic full English. As usual, Karen had forgone the unhealthy fried bread, replacing it with wholemeal, buttered toast. She accosted the waitress to insist the butter, not margarine, was spread when the toast was cold so she could check if the layer was thick enough. She could apparently judge its quality by the colour.

If Karen could have whims and fancies, so would Amy. She declined the black pudding in place of an extra sausage after she had checked the type and size of the sausage. She would also require extra beans and no tomato as the tinned ones were sharp. Emma just wanted it all and we knew she was light-headed by the way she held her knife and fork on end as if they were needed to prop her up. Mo had ordered an extra portion of sauté potatoes and we knew she would share them, partly to ease the guilt as Amy would be sure to roll her eyes and pat her stomach putting us all to shame before she pinched one or two.

My goodness, it didn't disappoint when it arrived. The extra-large, white oval plates did this British classic justice. Simple but scrumptious and cooked to perfection. Free-range eggs, butcher's thick-cut bacon, local pork and apple sausages, black pudding, fried farmhouse bread, homemade hash browns, sauté potatoes, button mushrooms, tomatoes and baked beans. The veggie options looked delicious too. Heaven on a plate.

We sat in silence as the task in hand, though delectable, was a mammoth one. Surely our hunger would be well and truly satisfied and we wouldn't need to eat for the rest of the day? After all, the portions were massive. As well as enjoying the food, we marvelled at the view that we knew we would never tire of. Perhaps things were looking up?!

I kept one eye on Karen and I knew the others were also keeping tabs. I had noticed her scanning her plate and gingerly poking her food. We knew she was trying to find fault but not today, everything was perfect. The only thing left was the mushrooms on Mo's plate.

'I just can't face them,' she sighed.

'They're definitely normal button ones,' said Amy with a burp.

'I realise that!' Mo replied defensively. She arched her eyebrows and tightened her lips as she glared at Amy.

'Drink plenty as we have to provide urine samples later,' she reminded us, eager to change the subject.

As it turned out, we were about to be entertained which was good timing as it prevented any post-food arguing. The perfect end to a well and truly scrumptious breakfast. This was turning out to be a memorable last day of our holiday and it felt justified.

We deserved it after all that had happened.

# CHAPTER 24

A busker had appeared from nowhere. She was setting up on the flat rocks opposite.

Though people watching was a favourite pastime of ours, on this Monday morning people were actually few and far between. The earlier rush outside the café was over. We welcomed the distraction as the eating had rendered us near useless, to say we were slumped was an understatement. Amy was stretched out on a spare couch. The mega amount of food had been a compromise for even the most accomplished eaters.

'I wonder what instrument she's gonna play?' said Mo, directing the question at Amy to motivate her. It definitely wouldn't be the guitar as all she had was an old, battered suitcase and a rucksack on her back.

'I love the suitcase,' remarked Emma.

It was indeed extraordinary. Although very worn and tattered, even from this distance we could see that it was soft leather. Weathered over time, its history would be a tale worth hearing. The catches glinted in the sunlight, they looked antique and were undoubtedly expensive. I could see that Emma was itching to get a closer look. She loved anything old, that's probably why she'd taken up with us.

We all started trying to guess what instrument she was going to play. She was an attractive woman, hippyish, maybe our age or slightly younger, it was hard to say. Her skin was tanned and somewhat weathered like the suitcase, exposure to the elements had aged her perhaps.

'No liver spots,' whispered Karen.

'She's younger than us, I reckon. Well, some of us,' she corrected herself as she eyed up Emma's younger, unblemished skin.

Sensing the stares, Emma piped up with one of her favourite sayings, 'There are no wrinkles on a balloon.' She looked uncomfortably bloated as she loosened her belt and puffed out her cheeks.

We were all struggling to finish our coffees and the homemade, chocolate-coated shortcake biscuits that had arrived, compliments from the café.

'There's no rush,' stated Amy, sensing the dilemma. 'Besides, I'd love to hear her play. I'm sure some of you will be hungry in half an hour, especially as there's all-butter shortcake on offer,' she added, scowling at Karen. 'Besides, no one's waiting to be seated.'

'We can offer her a bacon sandwich and a coffee,' suggested Liz. 'Mind you, she looks like a vegetarian.'

I feared Karen would give a lecture on stereotyping but not today, she had other things on her mind. All eyes were focused on the suitcase as there was another black case inside which she was opening.

'Flute!' Amy said quickly before anyone else.

It became obvious that she was a very accomplished musician. The song she played was magical but it edged on eerie as there was something about the melody that was giving me not only goosebumps but the creeps. Certain parts of the tune reminded me of the song that we had heard in the house.

Lack of sleep and all this sea air must've been heightening my imagination. I glanced around at the others to see if there was any reaction. They were all engrossed and smiling. No startled looks.

Jill had gone out to offer her a coffee and a sandwich. She was sitting next to her on the rocks and I decided to join her. The wind carried the music, it seemed to whistle in harmony with the notes. Several onlookers had gathered to enjoy it. It was mesmerising.

I glanced down at the intriguing suitcase, making the most of the close-up view. I couldn't believe what caught my eye. I must surely be delirious. A faded address label remained attached to the case. It was hanging by a tatty piece of string and fluttered in the wind. I could just make out the address which was written in faint, block capitals: WINDY PASSAGE.

My heart skipped a beat and I tugged at Jill's sleeve. My eyes directed her to follow me inside. I rushed into the café, my excitement undermining discretion. By the time I had blurted out what I had seen, the busker had disappeared.

'Where'd she go?' shouted Amy in a panic as she raced outside like a headless chicken escaping from a butcher's shop.

'She just shoved everything in the case and rushed off,' exclaimed Mo in disbelief.

We paced up and down outside but there was no sign of her. It was as if she had just vanished into thin air.

# CHAPTER 25

## 'Lisa'

Lisa made a hasty getaway, to put it mildly. Her feathers had been well and truly ruffled. She couldn't quite make it out but those women were up to something. They had that look about them, nosy parkers, troublemakers. Well, she had been called a few of those things in the past. They must think she was stupid, down-and-out, homeless and living on the streets.

The dumb blonde had made it blatantly obvious, the way she'd dragged her dozy friend back into the café and that little skinny one looked as high as a kite, bobbing her head up and down like a demented meerkat. At least they'd bought her a coffee. Overreaction again? Her ugly paranoia was back with a vengeance. It domineered and controlled her life on a daily basis, that and the wine and fags.

She ripped the address label from the suitcase and tried to steady her trembling hands as she rolled herself a joint. 'Geez, I'm a bag of nerves,' she cursed as she rubbed her hands along her Steinway piano, billowing dust into the shaft of sunlight that dared to creep through the gap in the curtain.

Lisa was a high-calibre classical pianist but you couldn't play a piano on the seafront. Well, she had actually, many years ago, in front of thousands but those days were long gone. The only stabling influence was music, her never-ending love. It calmed and relaxed her more than any drug. Now it was her only pleasure, well, that and the pot. Wine wasn't worth it as it caused such terrible hangovers.

The flat was dark and dingy and hidden away at the back of an ugly building. There was no nice view so she kept the curtains closed. The living space was tiny. There was barely room to move as most of it was taken up with musical instruments. They made up the bulk of her possessions and that suited her. She glanced at the Gibson in the corner. The lump in her throat came instantaneously but the tears didn't pool in her eyes anymore. They had dried up eventually. The guitar was a painful reminder of a gift that she didn't get to give. She wished that she had taken the old, crappy acoustic that he had loved as that was his soulmate and it was also doused in his DNA. She wondered where it had gone and that despair made her heart heavy with sadness and she felt deep aching regret. It was probably alone and discarded in some musty loft, just like herself.

In all honesty, she knew that her life had been privileged in many aspects and financially that continued as her inheritance was increasing each month. It was a measly amount that she took to live off and some months in the summer she survived solely off the busking. Money was the only thing she could thank her parents for and that was only appreciated of late as it allowed her to do what she wanted.

She was a free spirit but before they had died she'd had no control. Everything surrounding her upbringing had revolved around money. The only good thing, she reminded herself, was the music lessons and the access they gave her. She was almost certain that she would never have become a classical pianist of such stature without the money or the expensive private tutors, even the praise and encouragement had been bought and the latter was what ate into her more than anything else.

Had her success all really been, as she suspected, due to advantageous social and financial circumstances and privileges she had been afforded? Or was she born with talent and would have achieved it anyway, like Tony? Even when his name popped into her head, the thought was tinged with menace and anger. Love was a feeling long gone, she kidded herself. She had only known it for that short period of her life and it had literally disappeared overnight.

They had moved into Windy Passage on a cold January morning. The new year held hopes and ambitions for them both and the characterful house with such striking views would surely inspire creativity and maximise their music-making. It had and the year had got off to a promising start. Tony had written a song in the first month and his lyrics had improved tenfold.

Things were looking up on her side as well. Her diary had been nearly fully booked. The concerts provided a modest but steady income ensuring the rent and the bills could be paid. Besides, if things got tight she could always rely on her parents to bail her out. Moving down south had been a means of escape but as many of the concerts were in London she would need to stay over. She could just about tolerate that if it meant keeping them sweet.

The house was everything that they had hoped for. It soon became a big part of their lives, entwined with their personalities, well, certainly hers. They had discussed the peculiarity on several occasions. The way the atmosphere and the air inside seemed to affect their moods. It was the wind in the hallway, they had eventually figured out. Tony had found it creepy but she loved it. It was exciting. Eventually, she could almost read its strength and mood. It seemed to affect their temperaments or was it their actions and moods affecting the wind? She never got to find out. It didn't bear thinking about.

There was definitely something very odd about Windy Passage. The hallway seemed to have a mind of its own or, at least, someone else's. The house must harbour secrets, they had agreed one night after too many drinks and a row. The next day they decided to delve into its history but, unfortunately, they had never got the chance to finish what they started.

Tony was reading an old book he had found in a tatty, wooden trunk in the hallway. It had more than likely belonged to the house's owner, Mr Farhat. The book looked ancient and was on Tunisian history. Tony must have turned the corner, a habit she loathed, as her eyes were drawn to a particular page. Though the text was in Arabic, there were notes in the margins in English. The remarks were scrawled in faded pencil and had probably been written a long time ago.

The words 'windy passageway' instantly grabbed her attention and she felt sure that's where the strange name of the house had come from. She had become engrossed in the book and only glimpsed the next page as the horn from the taxi beckoned her away. There was a black and white sketch of a man lost in a sandstorm. The words pencilled in on the margins said 'Saharan dust and spirits' and, intriguingly, there was a set of latitude and longitude coordinates next to the words 'ley lines' which were underlined.

She had just managed to grab the piece of paper which fell from the book. It was more roughly scribbled notes but these were in pen. Tony's handwriting. He had obviously begun delving into the house's history in earnest which pleased her. She read what he had written as she sat in the taxi en route to the train station:

'Bedouins were superstitious about a certain area in the Saharan desert, thus the myth had become a traditional tale passed down the generations. The locals often shared the tale with tourists who lapped it up. A particular area in the desert was to be avoided, not only because of the strong winds but because the legends told of spirits that could tap into minds and induce madness. Only very few people had ever returned from this strange place, those that had told of a blood-red sky and a ferocious sandstorm. The mysterious shapes in the sand that they supposedly saw were put down to delirium and hallucinations, most probably due to dehydration. The name of this place, shunned by all but fools, was in Arabic. Its nearest translation into English was 'windy passageway'.

Her concert commitments meant she was spending more time away and looking back now Tony must have got bored or even lonely. There had been several complaints from the weird man next door so he had stopped practising in the evenings which she knew was when he felt most inspired. She had agreed it was a good idea when he announced he would play the guitar a couple of nights a week at the local pub down the hill. In retrospect, it had been a big mistake. They couldn't get enough of him and he soon had weekends as a regular booking. His sessions were drawing in the tourists as well as the locals.

She rolled another spliff as she knew what was coming. The memories brewed like a dark storm. There was no freezing wind to blast in here like it had in that hallway, sometimes calming her but other times provoking the pent-up anger to unleash itself, destroying anything in its path.

At the end of the day, she had been the fool and not the stupid barmaid that she had hardly noticed. Not until that last fateful night when his shocking revelation had actually sunk in. After all the handouts she'd given him, the encouragement, the love, the sex. It had all meant nothing. He had discarded her for the pretty woman next door. As usual, she was livid. The re-run of the events took a greater toll each time. More pot, more wine, and more grey hairs. She had actually not thought about it for weeks. It was those bloody women and that old, manky address label that had kicked it off again.

When she thought back now with a relatively sober mind, she had noticed something before he told her. That Saturday night when he played the love song, his greatest achievement so far. She thought he was just glancing up at the bar but now she knew better. That look in his eyes wasn't passion for the song, the little bitch had been smiling and returning the glances. Looking back now, the memory was vivid. Their eye contact had been blatantly and painfully obvious.

She lazed on her Eames sofa and let the spliff work its magic. Its analgesic effects would numb the pain and take away the guilt. She would open that vintage cabernet sauvignon later and by the evening it would all be forgotten like a bad dream. As she relaxed, her mind wandered to finish what was inevitable...

They'd had a few red wines after he finished playing that night. He was inundated with compliments which he had appreciated but had also felt embarrassed by. Attention was not something he coveted as he was not a vain man but instead quite private and shy. That vulnerability had been one of the most attractive things about him, as well as the natural good looks, she admitted with reluctance. She considered herself far too sophisticated to succumb to the charms of a handsome man. Her needs were far deeper.

As it turned out, he was shallow and weak, must have been, to fall for the charms of an attractive barmaid.

Those words were bitter and overly-exaggerated in her mind. Her remorseful thoughts reflected on her face, the wrinkles and lines were unforgiving, callous, hence the mirror was covered. Her reflection had been denied an appearance of late; a stark reminder of her continual suffering that was too cruel to bear.

It was dark when they walked home that September evening, the earlier blood-red sunset had disappeared like a fire doused by the rain. It had poured down but, thankfully, it had stopped in time for the walk home. The chill in the air was reminiscent of autumn evenings to come, its coldness was heightened as the sea breeze was bitter. She held onto him for comfort and warmth and she sensed it immediately. He almost pulled away, his body was tense and his stride increased like he wanted to leave her behind. The moonlight painted the sky a steel-grey toning down the stars, their twinkles just visible but somewhat subdued. It was the huge clouds that domineered. They were black without the sunlight. Their intimidating shapes towered above like monsters, reflecting the mood that was brewing below.

Her annoyance gained momentum, as did his ascent of the hill. He was gradually getting further away. The lactic acid built up in her leg muscles as the hill took its toll. She stopped to catch her breath and the anger took hold. He was looking back now, his expression full of loathing then pity. It was a face she didn't recognise and she knew what was coming.

She noticed his footsteps in the red sand that glimmered like glitter beneath the old door lamp. The wind howled through the hallway, sweeping in the sand and red dust. By the time she entered the house, he was sitting at the table. Perhaps to give them both courage, he'd poured two neat whiskeys. An error of judgement that would haunt them both. The air in the hallway was freezing, though the heating was on. She left her jacket on as it was so cold. His voice was colder still.

'I'm moving out,' he said as she entered the room. The features on his face had softened and his eye contact showed a drop of caring. It stunk of sympathy, which riled her up further but she was used to performing. Her next move came easily, especially with the whiskey to dampen her real feelings. She stopped him before he began another sentence. His explanation was irrelevant.

She downed the whiskey in one shot and poured herself another. He had hardly touched his. Her temper flared inside as he rounded the table and touched her arm with fondness. The passion they shared had gone, replaced instead with commiseration. A feeling that she had never experienced nor longed to.

'I was thinking the same,' she said suddenly. Her words came from nowhere. They were fake. It was the drink talking which brought an appropriate smile. 'I miss London, the buzz, the people. It's dead here, boring! Our relationship has run its course, best to part as friends.' She just about managed to hide the bitter tone and prevent slurring her words. The alcohol had kicked in big time and the room was swaying which wasn't surprising as she'd had well over the limit at the pub. He looked slightly dejected as he retreated in silence to the other room with his guitar in tow.

She sat in the window seat and lit a cigarette. She would never normally smoke inside but what the fuck! 'Desperate times call for desperate measures,' she said aloud as she took a drag.

Outside painted a bleak picture and mirrored her true feelings. She was desolate. Clouds covered the moon and stars, they were low and shielded the lights from the village. There was nothing to see but blackness, even the lighthouse, the beacon of safety, its soothing flicker obscured.

She poured herself another drink, fully aware that the level in the bottle was fast diminishing. He was sitting in the lounge when she passed through the hallway. She narrowly avoided slipping on the sand that had blown in through the letterbox. The wind had picked up and was howling like she was inside. Its freezing blast chilled her nose and fingertips like a winter frost. If only it had sobered her up. Her fingers and toes felt frost-bitten as she huddled in the foetal position in a cold, empty bed. The shivering was replaced by heaving sobs but the wind hid the sound of her sorrow and, thankfully, she soon passed out and escaped from the misery that had engulfed her.

It was heat and nausea that woke her. She realised she was alone in the bed. Cruel reality soon came flooding back, as did the tears. The ache and emptiness were far greater than the pulsating pain in her head so she staggered to the door to call him and confess her true feelings. She hated him earlier but she loved him now. She steadied herself in the darkness and edged towards the bedroom door which was slightly ajar. At that very moment, he was nearing the top of the stairs saying words she'd never hear from him again, 'I love you.'

He had his phone to his ear and a smile on his face. A glass of whiskey in his other hand.

She felt pure hatred as she stumbled through the doorway towards him.

The warm air from the bedroom clashed with the icy wind that was howling up the stairs. The noise was feral.

The shock startled him. The smile on his face disappeared as he teetered on the edge before stumbling backwards. The tortuous look of despair she saw as he perished would be etched on her soul forever. She must have blacked out as she didn't wake until the next morning and by then it was well and truly over. The red she saw then was purplish, Latvian red. There was no sand, just congealed blood covering most of the hallway.

# CHAPTER 26

We had the inclination but, unfortunately, not the time to investigate the strange woman as we were already running behind schedule. It was annoying to say the least as it was too much of a coincidence. Surely there must be a connection?

'She can be added to the weekend's mysterious happenings. We certainly have a long list of strange things to tell the police,' proclaimed Amy.

Jill paid the bill and we left a generous tip and thanked the waitress.

'We'll be back,' I said and I knew that we would as I felt sure that both the woman and the suitcase had answers.

The car seats seemed to groan in protest, presumably at the extra weight. Amy glared fervently at Emma's backside which looked like it had doubled in size. I noticed my stomach had done the same. I would much rather be pear-shaped than apple, it was healthier as well. There was a lot more tugging of seat belts and we were definitely more squashed together than we were on Friday. What further evidence did we need? I could sense a spiel about dieting was on the horizon and an argument for certain.

'No toilet stops, we need full bladders,' Karen reminded us. 'We can ask to do urine samples as soon as we get there.'

'We should be there in about half an hour,' I reminded her. 'After all, it's only about ten miles away.'

It appeared to be well organised when we arrived at the police station. They were actually expecting us which hopefully meant that we wouldn't have to wait to be seen.

It was probably the most exciting case they had dealt with in a long while. There was no denying it wasn't interesting.

We were assigned to a detective constable who seemed pleasant enough and was certainly very keen. He had a very familiar look about him but I couldn't quite put my finger on who he reminded me of. The others were staring as well, especially Amy. His attire was smart casual, the skinny jeans stood out as, amongst other things, they overemphasised the size of his feet. I noticed Karen eyeing up just that before her eyes ran up his inside leg. Although his physique was gangly, there was something about him that was positively attractive. He was certainly very animated, the slight bulge of the eyes and his long neck exaggerated the effect. Amy was taken in immediately, she seemed to mirror his every move. Long-lost brother maybe? There was chemistry in the air and I noticed her jittering was attracting his attention.

'One of my kind,' I imagined him thinking.

Karen was standing with her legs crossed, trying to drop a hint. She was never subtle. In the end, she cleared her throat and interrupted him. He tore his gaze from Amy. His side profile revealed slightly bucked teeth and a dent in his roman nose. He had a good head of thick, curly black hair and was cleanly shaven, no beard, which made a nice change. He reeked of masculinity, maybe that's what we were missing.

'Would it be possible to provide urine samples first?' Karen half enquired, half insisted. 'Only, we've been on a long car journey.'

'Ten miles!' Amy started to say in a disbelieving tone before I cut her short with a dig in the back.

He flushed from the neck upwards and appeared quite bemused as he fiddled with his lime green tie and opened the file in front of him. It was plain to all that he wasn't up to speed on the investigation and Karen spotted it like a hawk. There was no mercy, not even for a man that had captured our attention in such a curious manner.

Before she could cash in on his weakness, he rushed off with the file in a fluster towards a woman PC.

'Gone to do his homework,' whispered Rachel.

'Ah, give him a chance!' pleaded Amy. 'It's a police station, not an antenatal clinic.'

He spoke softly to his colleague. It was an unfortunate habit and I was sure it was unintentional but he appeared to look down his nose every time he spoke. His nostrils flared wildly. He gestured to us to wait as he ushered the policewoman into his office slamming the door behind them.

'He's telling us to wait a minute,' said Amy, picking up on the sign language as if she was the only one that could understand him.

'Well, I can't wait much longer,' groaned Emma walking up and down with her knees together. She had drunk two bottles of water in the car and obviously never kept up her pelvic floor exercises.

'Delay tactics, more like, whilst he familiarises himself with the case,' said Karen with irritation.

A few minutes later, the policewoman returned to us with sample bottles and all was forgiven. She stomped over to the desk arrogantly, 'Can you order some more of these piss pots,' she said to the receptionist whose eyes were glued to her computer screen. 'That lot,' she said as she jerked her head in our direction, 'have cleared us out.'

'Magic mushrooms,' she scoffed, then tutted.

The afternoon flew by as the statement taking and other formalities ran smoothly.

'What do you think will happen at Windy Passage?' I enquired as we were about to leave. His blush was fierce, a vein on his temple pulsed. That name definitely conjured up odd images for most people. Karen responded to his blank look with petulance.

'She means the house,' she snapped impatiently. She had no time or sympathy for his embarrassment. However, we knew he was very limited in what he could tell us so we didn't expect much of an answer.

'Looks like it was a cat under the floorboards,' he stuttered. 'That's our forensic guy's first impression.'

'Aw, that's terrible,' Emma replied. I could see that her eyes were already brimming with tears. We all sighed and I knew we were upset and disgusted as cruelty to animals was hated by all. There was never, under any circumstances, an excuse. That was one subject we had never needed to debate. Mind you, there had been lots of arguments over the years about vegetarians and vegans.

We were soon cruising down the motorway. Depending on the level of traffic, we would be home in about an hour. The other car was soon far behind us, a mere speck in the distance. Karen had put her foot down as usual. Her competitiveness was rife where driving was concerned and Fleetwood Mac's 'The Chain' had riled her up. Despite her determination, she drove safely and just within the speed limit...most of the time!

It was just as well that it had been an easy journey on Friday and that we were all familiar with the route as there had been a fair few rows in the past when Karen had been the lead driver. Her fear of being overtaken, which according to Amy stemmed from her being overtaken by a Smart car, invariably led her to lose the other car. Thankfully, the drive home was straightforward, mostly motorway, so we could all relax. Mo had fallen asleep in the back and was snoring gently. Though dissimilar, it reminded me of the snoring I had heard on the first night.

'Did anyone hear that snoring on Friday night?' I tentatively enquired.

'I consider any snoring strange,' answered Amy with disinterest.

Mo opened one eye.

'It sounded just like Cheyne-Stokes breathing,' she muttered. 'Poor Jill's worse than me now!' Her words petered out as her dozing resumed. I knew it wasn't Jill. The noise had come from downstairs and she told us that she hadn't slept there. Even though the perpetrator was in custody, there were still lots of things that didn't add up, so I knew there was plenty we needed to discuss as a group.

'I find it atrocious that he intended to actually drug us!' Karen stated with a wave of fiery anger that I was sure we all felt but were holding back.

'Well, at least we will find out what those pills were. Psychedelics of some sort I suspect, most likely LSD,' I said with abhorrence.

'I kept seeing a stain at the bottom of the stairs,' confessed Amy suddenly, her usual animated self returned as if the memory had stoked a fire.

'I saw that as well!' we all said in unison.

Mo was awake now, unable to ignore the revelations that began emerging. Was it reality I wondered or had the booze, excitement and the mushrooms muddied the waters? Would we ever find out the truth?

'There was definitely a figure at the top of the stairs,' Mo stated. Her tone was serious and we daren't argue. We didn't need to as we all believed her. I did for sure. I would never forget the lingering presence I felt in the air every time I had walked down the hallway.

Considering how it had all transpired, I genuinely believed it was there to help us and it had.

Surely someone else had seen the misty illumination just before the man emerged from the loft? There were three of us upstairs. I couldn't believe that they all denied seeing any such thing. I would broach the subject at our next get together, that's for sure.

'He must have mixed those shrooms in with the mushrooms,' reasoned Amy.

'We will find out for sure when we get the results from our urine samples,' Karen added. 'Hopefully there will still be traces of psilocin.'

I wasn't as confident that we'd get the results we wanted as it was over 24 hours after ingestion.

'The creepy crawlies, not forgetting the maggots, must have been planted on Saturday when we were out,' she continued with despair.

'The spider was in the bathroom on Friday,' I admitted. 'Emma saw it that night, didn't she Mo?'

There was no reply. She had shut her eyes again, probably to block out the madness or to mull over rational explanations like I knew we all invariably would. We carried on in silence, at least Karen had the road to concentrate on.

Darren, as we now knew he was called, must have had some terrible issues. There would be a story behind his actions for sure. There must be a reason that he had been driven to such extreme, shocking behaviour. At the very least he would get help with his mental health and that would be the best outcome. His desperate actions were probably a cry for help. After all that Sue had endured, she had been sympathetic and I admired that.

I was sleepy now and struggled to keep my eyes open. I gave in eventually and let the drone of the traffic lull me. My mind wandered further...

The mysterious aftershave. I had smelt it in the graveyard yesterday evening when we saw the groundsman by the headstone. We had followed the smell to the house.

I must have drifted off to sleep but a familiar voice in the distance woke me.

'There was a ghost in that house!' It was Karen. She was talking loudly to get our attention and she was deadly serious. Her hands gripped the wheel so tightly that her knuckles were white, as was her face. Before she had time to shed light on her startling declaration, the ring of a mobile startled us. It was Karen's, which was hands-free. It was Emma calling from the other car.

'I'm gutted about the animals that got caught up in all of this,' she began. 'I hope he gets charged appropriately. The RSPCA needs to be informed.'

'I've been thinking,' she continued. Amy raised her eyebrows but declined to comment. 'Seagulls can be a nuisance but that one was quite tame, it certainly didn't deserve to be poisoned. Even the spider has upset me,' she spluttered. 'It probably won't survive outside.'

'It's the cat that has really unsettled us,' cringed Liz in the background.

'What sort of person kills a domestic cat?'

'We need a meeting this week,' shouted Rachel above the crackles as the phone cut off.

We had arranged to meet for breakfast at our favourite café on home ground. As Karen dropped us off one by one, a safe onward journey was wished by all. We knew for sure we would all enjoy a glass of wine and a group chat that evening. We deserved it after the stressful weekend we'd had. Our tenth anniversary had definitely been memorable, to say the least.

It wasn't long before I was home and it was a great feeling. I smiled at the view as I walked up the winding path to the quaint 18th-century cottage that I adored. The garden was stunning, a true higgledy-piggledy cottage garden. I never ceased to be amazed at how many plants and trees I had managed to fit into such a modest space alongside the resident wildflowers that had self-seeded for hundreds of years. It was glorious, a haven for wildlife just as I had intended. I realised how lucky I was as Roy and the dogs rushed out to greet me.

It was stressful and surreal as I recounted the weekend's events to Roy over supper, playing down some parts as I knew he'd be annoyed at my frivolousness. He was flabbergasted, in shock like myself, and I am sure that he thought the story was grossly exaggerated as he knew that was one of my many faults along with an overactive imagination. In fact, I'd even been known to make things up. He looked stunned so I left him with his beer to take it all in and I took my glass of wine into the garden.

I sat on the wooden bench under the olive tree. Dusk was approaching but a few lonesome bees buzzed in the foxgloves foraging for supper, eager to ensure that the last rays of sunlight would not be wasted. A hummingbird hawkmoth hovered above the jasmine trying to guide its proboscis into the tiny white flowers. Though there was plenty to entertain me, I kept looking at my phone. I was anxious to hear from the others but I didn't want to disturb them. The sun had almost disappeared but tonight the air was warm so I sat a bit longer, quietly thinking.

It wasn't surprising that no one had messaged, as what a tale we all had to tell. I kept thinking about the

214

house and the strange occurrences, most of which could be put down to human interference. I half hoped the police would provide some rational answers but I knew deep down that the house held a secret. I had felt it in the wind in the passageway and I'd seen it in the busker's eyes, heard it in her music. And what were the chances of someone falling downstairs and their carotid artery being pierced by a shard of glass? Bullshit!

I would suggest a summer trip at our next get-together. I felt sure Karen would be onside and Amy, as all things considered we'd had a great weekend. Full of all of our favourite things: laughter, adventure, food and drink. Our friendships were stronger than ever, so I hoped we'd all be on board.

I was just about to go inside when the phone chirped. It was a message from the group chat. Emma was sending the group selfie taken in the window seat on Saturday night.

We all looked beautiful, exceedingly happy and a wee bit tipsy. It was certainly a stunning photo, the best one yet. Thumbs up to Emma!

The black storm clouds were gathered behind us ensuring we took centre stage. The blood-red lining looked like a hand-drawn addition as it outlined us perfectly. The outlandish, sparkly diamante shoes drew my eyes downwards for a second and I smiled at something so inconsequential. The sky beyond the clouds was gold and my eyes couldn't help but wander to what the flash had uncovered...

I quivered at the mere thought and my mind raced. The simple task of zooming in was hampered by my now trembling hands. The bright outline was distinct, surely unmistakable?

It revealed what must be a reflection in the window. The figure of the man stood behind me, looking over my shoulder. He was tall, his liquid-gold physique was striking. His bone structure promised handsome features. I felt sure that I'd seen him somewhere before. His smile melted my heart. He looked happy, content at the very least.

I could hardly contain myself as I hurriedly typed with one finger.

'ZOOM IN!

Can anyone else see it?

The spirit…

The spirit in the glass….'

# APEROL SPRITZ

**100ml Aperol**

**150ml Prosecco**

**Soda water, to top up**

Add the above to a large glass filled with ice cubes.

Garnish with a slice of orange.

Enjoy!

# ALABAMA SLAMMER

**28ml Disaronno or your amaretto of choice**

**28ml Sloe gin**

**28ml Southern Comfort**

**Orange juice, to top up**

Add the above to a large glass filled with ice cubes.

Garnish with a slice of orange and a glacé cherry.

Enjoy!

# KAREN'S MUSHROOM STROGANOFF

**2 garlic cloves (optional)**
**1 large onion**
**4 celery sticks**
**Butter (lots)**
**350g chopped mushrooms (mixed, not magic)**
**1 tbsp flour**
**150-300ml water**
**1 tsp Marmite**
**142ml sour cream**
**FRESH chopped thyme**
**Salt and pepper**

Sauté onions, garlic and celery in butter.

Add flour.

Add water, Marmite and thyme.

Add mushrooms.

Simmer for 20 mins.

Add sour cream 5 mins before serving.

Garnish with fresh herbs and a swirl of cream. Serve on a bed of wild rice.

**N.B.** All amounts are approximate.

# About the Author:

Julie Higgins (Venner) enjoyed a rewarding 35-year career in the NHS as both an intensive care nurse and a midwife before rediscovering her love of writing following early retirement.

Inspired by a wealth of experience in the NHS and the annual adventures she embarks on with her real-life ex-colleagues, she decided to write a novel that followed a similarly eccentric band of best friends on a fictional trip that none of them would be able to forget...no matter how much alcohol they drank! The Spirit in the Glass is her debut novel.

Born and bred in The West Country, Julie lives in West Huntspill, Somerset, with her husband and two dogs. If you enjoyed reading about the gang's shenanigans, please consider leaving a review.

Printed in Great Britain
by Amazon

60961103R00137